ELVES
The Adventures of Nicholas:

THE GRID OF AGONY

and

THE FIELD OF LOVE

By

V. Vernon Woolf, Ph.D.

Books by Victor Vernon Woolf, Ph.D.

Holodynamics: How To Develop and Manage Your Personal Power
The original text

The Dance of Life
Transform your world NOW! Create wellness, resolve conflicts and learn to harmonize your "Being" with Nature.

The Holodynamic State of Being: Manual I
Advocates a course in life that unfolds one's fullest potential for the individual and for the planet.

Presence in a Conscious Universe: Manual II
Detailed training in achieving the state of being present, aligning with one's Full Potential Self, bonding with others, transforming holodynes and unfolding of potential.

Field Shifting: The Holodynamics of Integration: Manual III
Training exercises for integration of field of information from the past, present and future through the relive/prelive processes.

Leadership and Teambuilding: The Holodynamics of Building a New World: Manual IV
The use of a Holodynamic approach within systems as in business and education.

Principle-Driven Transformation: The Holodynamics of The Dance of Life: Manual V
The principles, processes and stories that form the basis for teaching Holodynamics.

The Therapy Manifesto: 95 Treatises on Holodynamic Therapy
An outline of 95 findings from current sciences that apply to the theory and practice of therapy.

The Wellness Manifesto: 95 Treatises on Holodynamic Health
A declaration of findings from current sciences that apply to the health industry.

Elves: The Adventures of Nicholas: The Grid of Agony and The Field of Love
A science fiction story about time-traveling elves who live according to the principles and processes of Holodynamic consciousness and become involved in an intergalactic battle that sweeps a small boy, Nicholas Claus, into shifting the grid of agony into a field of love. How Christmas began.

Intimacy: Develop your Being of Togetherness: How to Create an Open, Dynamic, Effective, Intimate, Living Relationship with Someone You Love

Related Writings

Tracking: The Exploration of the Inner Space by Kirk Rector
The Ten Processes of Holodynamics by Kirk Rector

The above writings can be purchased at www.holodynamics.com/store.asp

ELVES

The Adventures of Nicholas:
The Grid of Agony and the Field of Love

By
Victor Vernon Woolf, Ph.D.

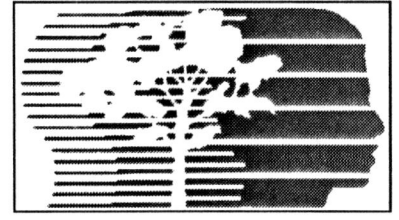

ELVES:
THE ADVENTURES OF NICHOLAS:
THE GRID OF AGONY AND THE FIELD OF LOVE

All rights reserved.
Copyright © 1995/2006 Victor Vernon Woolf, Ph.D.

Original Illustrations by the author
Cover by Debbie Drecksel
Design by Debbie Drecksel
Others by permission as noted

No part of the book may be reproduced or transmitted in any form or by any means, electronic or mechanical, including photocopying, recording, or by any information storage and retrieval system, without permission in writing from the publisher except for brief reviews or quotations for noncommercial use as permitted by copyright law.
For information address: Victor Vernon Woolf, Ph.D.
www.holodynamics.com

Library of Congress Cataloging-in-Publication Data

Woolf, Victor Vernon
Elves: The Grid of Agony and the Field of Love: The Adventures of Nicholas

Includes
ISBN 0-9746431-8-1 (pbk.)
1. Consciousness. 2. Christmas. 3. Science Fiction.
4. Self-Organizing Information Systems. 5. Quantum Theory.
6. Self Help. 7. Title.

PRINTED IN THE UNITED STATES OF AMERICA

Publisher: Victor Vernon Woolf, Ph.D.
823 South Sixth Street, Suite 100, Las Vegas, NV 89101

Additional copies of this text may be obtained directly through www.holodynamics.com
or from your local distributor.

TABLE OF CONTENTS

Chapter One: The Sleigh Ride   1

Chapter Two: The Black Stone Monastery   7

Chapter Three: The Griffs in the Pitts of Hell   23

Chapter Four: My Father's Workshop   31

Chapter Five: The Starship   41

Chapter Six: The Death of a Sender   57

Chapter Seven: The Delovian Galactic Council   67

Chapter Eight: The Birth of a Sender   73

Chapter Nine: The Rebirth of a Sender   79

Chapter Ten: The Crack in the Cosmic Egg   93

Chapter Eleven: Kris Kringle and the Black Crystal   109

Chapter Twelve: The Shifting of the Field   117

Chapter Thirteen: The Elfin Project   127

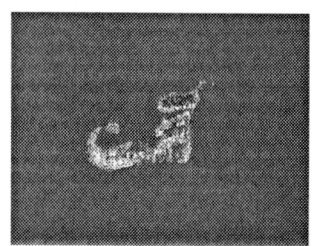

ELVES
The Adventures of Nicholas:

THE GRID OF AGONY

and

THE FIELD OF LOVE

"Open the portals of time. Seed the Grid of Agony with love. Shift the field from fear to love. Transform the past and create the future now. Be the Sender. The Grid of Agony grows. You will need more Senders. Call them. They will come. Let them gather together and transform the Grid of Agony into a Field of Love. Preserve life on this planet. All that is required, you have."

The Elf gently, so gently, removed his aged, three-fingered hands from my shoulders. Too much living in time had aged him. His great almond eyes held mine for a moment and, in that moment, I could see a thousand lives so clearly it was as though I had lived them as my own. Life after life after life and lesson upon lesson upon lesson swept before me as my mind leapt to the realization of love so profound, of peace so universal, it had woven the very fabric of time and space and birthed the source from which life sprang.

A river of light burst from my heart washing through every cell of my body; lifting, cleansing and transforming the ashes of my agony; freeing and centering me. Suddenly I was back again to the days of my youth working with my father in his toy shop, yet filled with an unspeakable joy.

As he turned to leave, his parting words echoed over and over in my heart; "You are the Sender. Send for the others." Then he was gone, his star ship dissolving into the vastness of inner space.

I am the Sender Nicholas, known as Santa. This is the story of my adventures with the Elves and of how they taught me to transform the Grid of Agony by seeding it with the Field of Love and saving life of planet Earth.

Chapter One

The Sleigh Ride

On the day before my sixth birthday, in the year 1482* my father, Hans Claus, had just finished work on a new sleigh. For weeks he had labored to master the curved front, the hand-carved sides and the detailed forging and shaping of the runners. Finally, when it was finished, I had to wait another whole day for the wood wax and bright red paint to dry.

The heavy snows, which covered the mountains surrounding our valley, were perfect for sledding. "How much longer, Father?" I would ask. "Not much, not much. Patience, my son," he would reply.

My father and I lived alone in a richly forested valley, secluded far beyond and above the village of Milan, in northern Italy. Here the mighty Alps begin their decent into the Mediterranean Sea and our only neighbors were the priests who lived five miles down the next valley at the Black Stone Monastery.

Father avoided any contact with the priests of the Monastery. It was because of what they had done to my mother during the inquisitions. But, on this day, nothing would stop us from taking the only really good sleigh run, even if it took us under the very shadows of their monolithic monastery.

"Do you have your pack ready?" he asked, as he gently lifted the bright red shiny new sleigh from its hooks over his workbench. I rushed to get my pack. "And don't forget your firelighter!" he insisted. At last, we were off.

Sentinel pines penetrated a solid blue sky as we worked our way up over the crest between our valleys. We reached the heavy-crusted snows that blanketed the mountaintops and the upper valley where the sun-basked ridges creaked under the weight of it. As we crossed the ridge, we came face-to-face with the ancient Black Stone Monastery. Dominating the entire side of the mountain, its great walls were topped with gothic figures peering down over the pristine valley below. It gave me the shudders.

My father hardly noticed. He was looking skyward. As I followed my father's gaze, a magnificent white hawk circled slowly in the air. Without a word, we passed over the ridge. Once in awhile we would pause to catch our breath and then we continued our struggle upward to reach the top of the run. I grew tired. "Father, can't we find another way to get up this mountain?" I asked. "How could it be done?" he replied.

"Couldn't we use a sail, like a boat?" I asked, just trying to figure it out. "Which way does the wind blow?" he queried. "Down the mountain," I moaned. I could sense his skepticism. I knew what was coming next. "Do you think the sail could carry us up if the wind blows down?" He raised his great bushy eyebrows as he glanced back at me. "Could we tack?" I joked.

"Ho, Ho, Ho. Keep on thinking," he mumbled. Then, after a few more yards of upward climb, I continued, "Could we get snow deer to pull us up?" He looked over at me with both eyebrows raised. "They are pretty small you know."

But I continued to think it out. "Still, they like the snow." We trudged on a few more yards. Finally, he continued as if drawn into the subject. "Well, how many snow deer would it take?" he asked as though he were really interested in the subject.

"Eight." It just came out of me. I just knew it was eight. So he kept right on with the subject. "And how would they get us to the top?" he asked.

"Well, maybe they could just fly. Yeah, that's how they could do it. Maybe we could fly in the sleigh." It was such a magical thought - and this was a moment for imagination. We were getting well up into the heavy snow and the field over which we climbed had leveled out so the going was a little easier. Imagination was a favorite way my father and I had of passing our time together.

"Well," said Father, "You'd have to be a Santa." "A saint?" I asked, truly befuddled. "Only they have the power," he said as he stopped to catch his breath. I sat down beside him as he dropped to the crusted snow.

"What is a Santa?" I asked as I lay back into the sun. "Someone who uses the power of love to do good." He said it as though he really knew. It was like my father, to know such things and I trusted in his words like they were manna from heaven.

"Can they really fly?" My mind was swirling with the possibilities. What if angels could fly? What if people could fly? His reply was like pushing me over a cliff. "If love required it, I guess they could do just about anything."

"I'd like that!" I said, lost in the flight of my own imagination. "Could I become a Santa?" The words just slipped out of me. He chuckled as he got to his feet. "If you had the faith you could even fly up a mountain." I, too, stood. We began to climb again and, like always, I began to hum a tune. Then I started making up words.

"Boom, boom, boom, boom. If birds can fly, and flies can fly... if clouds and moon and sun can fly, maybe someday, couldn't I? Boom, boom, boom, boom, boom." We climbed on, approaching the point where we could see our destination at the top of the run. I sang on, passing the time.

"If angels fly and arrows fly... if clouds and moon and sun can fly, maybe someday couldn't I? Boom, boom, boom, boom, boom. Maybe if a Santa, I could fly. Boom, boom, boom, boom. Booom Booommmm."

Then, I pointed to my father and said, "Your turn. Boom, boom, boom, boom..." He joined right in. "If rain can fly, and snow can fly... if rocks and sticks (I threw a piece of snow and father raised his eyebrow) can fly," he paused. I cut right in; "Then someday surely wouldn't I? Boom, boom, boom, boom, boom. Someday I'll be Santa and I'll fly! Boom, boom, boom, boom. Booom Boooommm!"

As we laughed and sang our way to the top of that long climb, the sound of our coming reverberated off the mountains and the heavy snows groaned and shifted under the impact of the sound of our voices. The sun-warmed, wet snowdrifts hung heavy over the crests. Even the sound of our passing may have caused them to be loosened but they loomed above us unnoticed in the joy of our being together.

We reached the pinnacle of the hill, turned the sleigh and tucked ourselves in. I remember how my father's long legs secured each side of me so I was safe and protected both by him and by the sleigh, which curved upward and inward, partially covering me at the front. Tucked in good and snug, I realized the moment had arrived.

"Forward launch!" laughed my father as we pushed off down the hill. The sleigh immediately picked up speed. We dashed down the hill leaning to the left and then to the right in our headlong flight. Down the ice-crusted mountainside we plummeted. Excitement pounded through me as we took to the air when our sleigh suddenly cascaded over a great hump.

"Ho, Ho, Ho. You can fly! You're a Santa! HO! HO! HO! Santa!" my father shouted over the rush of the wind in my ears. That jump was so long, I heard him gasp under his breath, "Oh ho, Santa!" while I was holding my breath, frozen for that moment in fright.

Time stood still. I flew as if forever. My father's shouts seemed to pass into a tunnel a long way away. I could hear him. "We are flying through the air. Ho! Ho! Ho!" but it was as in a dream.

"That's my Santa!" jarred me out of my fear trance. While everything seemed in slow motion, once we crunched back onto the ice, a surge of pure excitement took over. The magic of the moment became an infusion of fun and adventure and of being one with nature, the mountain, the sleigh and my father as we catapulted jump after jump down the hill flying toward the great shadow of the monastery.

I let go of my grip and raised my hands as the sleigh flew through the air on another big jump. "Look, Father! I'm a Santa. I can fly. I can fly. I'm a Santa!"

At that moment, a priest, dressed in black and situated high in the tower of the monastery, pulled the toll rope on the bell. The sound of the great gothic bell reverberated through the valley and bounced off the snow-laded mountain crests, shaking loose the fragile grip of the early winter snows. Branching off from the valley where we were sleighing, a great rumble announced the birth of an avalanche as the mountain shed the upper weight of its new, wet heavy, winter coat.

Down that branching side of the valley, hidden from our view and so unseen by my father or me, the wall of snow and debris swept toward us. My father sensed its presence too late. A huge tree, combined with several great snow boulders, caught on the crest of the avalanche and hurled down upon us in front of a tidal wave of snow.

My father tried to turn the sleigh but it was too late. Caught in the momentum, he was thrown into the air. I remember he screamed my name and scrambled to grab me, but he was tumbled by the snow and carried on the crest of the avalanche to be turned down into the underside of a giant pine rolling like a great jagged wheel across the crest of the snow.

"Nooooo!" I screamed as I instinctively clung on for dear life, crouched inside beneath the curved front the sleigh.

The sleigh and I were thrown into the air, plummeted up and down, sideways and crossways, riding the crest of the avalanche wave until we tumbled end over end to be dumped upside down at the bottom of a great ditch. Tons of snow must have flowed over me as I lost consciousness underneath the sleigh.

There was no light when I awoke. I must have had the breath knocked completely out of me. At first, I lay for some time in what must have been a semiconscious state. The first thing I remember was I couldn't breath. As I struggled to breathe, I tried to push the snow away from my face. To my relief, it gave way and I rested while I caught my breath. I was getting cold.

After a while, I pushed more snow away and made a little space for myself. As I kept pushing, I was surprised to find the snow gave way on the left side of my little space.

I kept pushing. It kept giving. I felt around and discovered I had created a small crawl space from under the sleigh into the end of what I knew not. It did not take me long to discover it must have been a sewer pipe coming from the monastery.

Chapter Two

The Black Stone Monastery

$\mathcal{F}$or my father, his worst nightmare was about to begin. He lay unconscious beneath the tree that had wrenched him from the sleigh. An ominous silence filled our separated worlds.

He was roused by snow falling on his face. His panic brought more snow and he almost suffocated until he got to his senses and then more carefully figured out which way was up. Slowly he dug his way through the branches of the tree, packing each space below him and beside him with the snow from above.

Waves of panic washed over him. As he finally emerged from the snow, his panic grew to almost consume him. "Nicholas! Nicholas!" he screamed over and over as he searched desperately through the valley of snow. Only the echoing silence of the white snow met his desperation.

The priests, for whom the bell had tolled high in their towering monastery, could not discern the words through the faintness of the echo. They had returned to their prayers.

As for me, the sewage pipe was made of old stone. I crouched on hands and knees as I crawled upward for some time in total darkness. Then I remembered I had a way to get a light! My father insisted I always wear my pack on my back when out in the woods. In it was my twirly – the fire-maker! Cramped as I was in such a small space, I squirmed and twisted and, after quite a bit struggle, I finally was able to get the pack off. In the total darkness, I groped around until I found my twirly, which was made of flint joined to a small flywheel. When I twirled it fast, it gave off sparks. It was for making fires outdoors.

When I twirled it in the sewer pipe, it threw off sparks that must have ignited the sewer gas. There were little puffs all along the pipe. It was scary. But I could see for a long way, even if for only a few seconds. The pipe seemed to go up forever.

I knew the small stream over which I crawled in the pipe must come from somewhere and, since I couldn't go back, I kept on going up the steep incline of the pipe. I was beginning to wonder if I might be trapped in this darkness forever when I came to an ancient stone grate across the pipe. I twirled my twirly and could see a larger underground tunnel on the other side. The grate was very old and, at first, it appeared solid. But, after shaking it for awhile, cramped as I was in the pipe, I got turned around and could put both my feet against it. I kicked and kicked as hard as I could and, finally, I could feel that part of it crumbled. I was able to kick and push and shift it enough to squeeze my way past and get into the tunnel. The ground was level! I didn't have to climb up anymore!

I groped around for some time, twirling my sparker and igniting the gases in great puffs. Finally, after some time, as I sparked my twirly, I spotted a shadow on the wall. Could it be a torch? It was just over the height of my head but, carefully feeling my way up the wall under it, I got hold of a notch and pulled myself up. With one hand I grabbed the ancient thing and swung out onto it. It collapsed under my weight and I crashed to the floor. I was not hurt but was covered with dust and debris. As I groped around in it, I found a bundle of cloth attached to a stick. I was right! It was an old torch. With my twirly and some careful fanning of the spark, I was able to light it so I could see. Never before had I realized how precious light was.

The passage was thick with spider webs. Spiders, rats and crawly cockroaches almost the size of my hand barely noticed my passing. Small gas puffing explosions occur each time I swing the torch near the water. I trudged along the side of the stream until I came to an old walkway crossing the stream. I stepped onto what looked like an ancient wooden bridge. As I put my weight upon it, it suddenly collapsed. In desperation, I thrust my arm back and tossed the torch across the stream as I plunged head first into the stream.

The first thing I noticed was that the stream was warm! As I rose to the surface, I gasped for air and began flailing my arms and feet in a desperate attempt to grab hold of the bank. Finally, I crawled out covered with grime. The torch lay on the other side of the stream! But I still had light! The only trouble was that my light was now on the other side of the stream.

The stream was too wide for me to jump, so I made my way to an arch and began to spider my way over the stream along a ridge of stones that held up the center of the archway. As I reached the keystone, I looked down over my shoulder into the water and almost fell from fright. Out of the darkness of the water, I saw a large slithery creature drawn to the light of the torch.

Its head and long backbone broke the surface of the water as I froze against the keystone arch. It looked around with what seemed like intelligent, reptilian eyes. I stayed frozen to my spot. Perhaps it was not seeing any motion that made it decide to finally submerge and I watched as its ripples continued on down the stream.

When I was sure it was gone, I scrambled like a spider from the keystone onto the walkway, ran to the torch and took off down the passage. But the creature was more cleverer than I thought. It had returned! Suddenly I heard it as it came lunging through the water toward me. I turned just in time to see it and dodged quickly into a side passage. The side passage was too narrow for it because its head crashed against the sides of the opening with a great "CRUNCH".

I stood almost paralyzed as it thrust itself against the stone pillars through which I had made my escape. I knew I was safe for the moment and then noticed I was covered with spider webs. I swatted and clawed away at them and then, with the beast still thrashing against the pillars, I looked around. Holding up the torch, I discovered myself surrounded by spaces cut back into the walls. In each space was something covered in dust and, as I drew the light closer to the one next to me, my light reflected off something white inside.

As I drew closer for a better look, I almost passed out when I realized I was looking down into the face of a human. A dead human! I must have screamed because the beast suddenly stopped crashing against the passageway and, as I spun to look at it, my light showed I was in a long passage filled with ledges. On each ledge was a skeleton covered in cloth.

My focus, however, was drawn to the reflection coming from the eye of the beast as it peered into the passage. I knew then that it was trying to figure out a way to get to me and so I turned and ran. Down the narrow passage, splashing my way through the small stream that ran between the coffins of stone, I sought only to escape. Little did I care that I was in the bowels of the Black Stone Monastery. I thrust my torch forward, burning off part of the webs as I ran. I did not realize, until some time later, that this was an ancient crypt, the burial grounds of the monastery. The bodies wrapped in rags, long mildewed into dust, with skeletons protruding from carved crevices and their shadowy resting places rising 15 feet up the walls meant little to me as I thrust myself further and further into the darkness.

At last I came to a place where the passage opened. It was filled with shadows of great stone piles of coffins. Dust and spider webs were everywhere. Under ordinary circumstances, I would be interested in the skeletons but now they looked like ominous centennials guarding the secrets of some ancient order. I wondered if the creature had eaten them all and placed them all in rows so it could remember its victims. I slowed to a walk.

I burned my way through the webbed passage, step by step, until I came to a fresh waterfall cascading into the stream. There I washed myself off and, to my surprise, the water was warm. I had no time to rest, however, because the Griff, for that is what I have since learned the mutant dragons were called, found its way up the stream by another passage. It was drawn by the light of my torch.

It turned into the inlet coming from the crypt and then it began to stalk me. At first I did not know it was there as I was fascinated at all the dead bodies and weird carvings on the passage walls. I was burning away the spider webs as I made my way along the path when, at one point the skeletons seem to come alive. I heard a deep moan and then I heard voices. I thought were coming from the dead because there was a great moaning sound. Then I heard a scream! Then another scream pierced through the walls. I almost fainted it was so scary. Then I realized there was also singing and talking.

I was so scared at one loud scream, I backed into a pile of coffins which, being piled so high, tipped over into the stream. As I turned my light toward the toppling coffins I was just in time to see the Griff rise from the shadows. I jumped back as the coffins cascaded down from their stacked position on the wall and a bunch of them toppled over onto the Griff. The collapse of the coffins raised such a clatter that I thought, for a moment, that the whole row of coffins might collapse.

I was about to run, not knowing where to go, when I glanced at the wall behind the coffins. There was an odd light shining through the darkness of the wall. The Griff seemed, at least temporarily, very securely buried, so I went over to see where the light was coming from, hoping to find a way out of this terrible place.

As I laid my torch down against the wall on the floor, I heard talking on the other side of the crypt wall! I knew the Griff was struggling to get free but I couldn't help lifting a little turn latch around which shone the light. It was rusted but finally I got it opened. There was a peephole under the latch!

Looking through the peephole, I peered into the largest room I had ever seen. It was filled with what at first I thought must be some sort of strange toys. Then I noticed they could only be for causing people pain. There were wrist shackles on the wall, a great iron coffin with huge spikes in it and among other contraptions, a great round barrel. A man was stretched upon the barrel with his hands and feet shackled. A small priest dressed in black stood by laughing in glee while the biggest man I ever saw turned a great handle which was attached to the barrel. The man on the "rack," as it was called, groaned in agony.

Two other people, whether male or female I could not tell for they were dressed in rags, hung from the walls suspended by chains on their wrists. Never had I imagined such a place of pain and agony.

In the midst of it all, the dwarf and giant were singing!

"Agony and pain, agony and pain,
People suffering, crying, sighing, lying, dying.
Agony and pain, agony and pain,
Ah, but what the gain? What the gain!
How despicable, how delectable!
Agony and paaaaaiiiiin!"

Suddenly the dwarf stopped and looked right at me. He didn't come over to the peephole but he immediately scurried out of the room. The giant unshackled the man's feet and wrists, hung him from the wall, and, with one last glance, he looked directly at my peephole and then followed the dwarf. I breathed a sigh of relief and leaned back against the wall to recover.

A chime drew my attention to another beam of light reflecting from a hole on the other side of the crypt. I made my way across the stream, jumping on the top of some of the coffins and avoiding the Griff trapped underneath as it still struggled to free itself.

I slid open the old rusty covering of the peephole. Putting my eye close to the hole, I peered into what seemed an even larger room. Great tapestries hung upon the walls and polished black marble covered the floor. In spite of the magnificence of it all, my eye was drawn to the center of the room where, raised on a white circular podium, was a magnificent white altar embedded with many colored crystals. At the very center of the altar was a golden, three-fingered hand reaching up and clutching a huge black crystal. From the crystal flowed a continuous stream of billowing darkness making everything look watery and sort of eerie.

Bending over the crystal was a man in a black hooded cloak. His arms raised heavenward, his eyes peering downward into the depths of the dark crystal and everything bristled with dark and sinister energy. The dwarf entered and, without pausing, joined the priest at the altar. As they peered into the crystal together, the dwarf suddenly looked up and turned toward my little peephole.

"Something threatens the source," he growled as to as he returned his gaze back into the blackened depths of the crystal.

"He is young. A young boy," murmured the priest. "But there is something strange about this one. Look at the glow about him. Could it be? If it is," he mumbled to himself, "Hmmmm, he may be a Sender! But look, he is only a boy!" The small dwarf-like priest raised his head.

"Capture him!" he growled. "We must contain his source!" Then, I watched as he bent over the dark crystal and I heard him say, almost to himself, "Only a Sender can threaten the void. We must capture him and convert him to the source!" Then he grabbed the larger priest by the arm and whispered, "If we convert him his energy will be transmuted." Malevolent, the larger of the two priests turned and walked to the side of the room where he pulled a great cord. A dozen priests immediately assembled.

"There is a boy who has escaped and is loose in the monastery. Find him and bring him to me. Be careful, brothers, for this boy may be very dangerous. Spare no effort. Find him!" commanded Malevolent.

Both the dwarf and the Malevolent drew close to the crystal ball. I was transfixed behind the wall, still peering through the peephole. As the two torturers looked into the crystal they must have seen me watching from behind the peephole because I heard the dwarf suddenly whisper:

"He is right behind that wall. Get him. Bring him to me." It was then I noticed his hand. It had only three fingers and they did not look like anything human I had ever seen. I was so fascinated I failed to notice the Griff. It had slipped out from under the pile of coffins and now was turning toward me.

Before I could think about it, Malevolent hurried out of the room and the dwarf, moving at great speed, suddenly shouted, "I will get him myself!" He scurried up behind one of the curtains, faster than a squirrel, and dropped down through a trap door. Almost instantly, he was in the passageway where, moments before, I had been looking through the peephole.

But I was on the move. I ran down that passage more scared than I had ever been in my life. Knowing the dwarf was close behind, I ran into the passage where the main underground river flowed. I scurried to my right and then, as I came to a side passage, I almost bumped into the Griff!

I threw my torch into the face of the creature, which was momentarily startled, and I dodged back into the crypt area into a cleft behind one of the caskets as the Griff darted away into the water. I stood very, very still; holding my breath as the dwarf flew by, looking toward the dying torch.

Failing to see me, the dwarf stepped quietly to the next passage and listened, slowly turning his slanting almond eyes up and down the passage, his pointed ears raised. Something made a noise in the water around the bend and the dwarf scurried off.

I spun around and took off, running down the very passage from which the dwarf had come. I could hear the priests coming from the other direction. I knew I would soon be trapped, so I climbed the wall where the dwarf had come down and found the little trap door. I climbed out and down behind the curtain. Malevolent and his followers were gone. I stood alone in the great hall.

I should have run from that place and never come back but I was spellbound by the wonder of the room and especially of the altar! Its center was more beautiful than anything I had ever seen.

I was always curious as a boy and, in spite of the danger all around me, I moved toward that altar awestruck by its strange and beautiful power. As I peered into the great black crystal held in place by the three-clawed hand made of gold, I can remember thinking, "What a toy!" And then I wondered "How does it work?" Knowing I could be discovered at any moment, still I could not resist the time to look deep into the crystal.

For a moment, it was as though it had a mind of its own, or it was a focus for my own, I knew not which. But I felt its power and was amazed as it began to gather about me, focusing and flowing through me. Almost too late, I noticed a door beginning to open into the room and I heard voices of priests. There was no place to hide except behind the altar of the crystal.

I sought to tuck myself in as best I could when suddenly a panel slid silently open. There was a small space and without looking I folded myself in and held as still as I could. Crouching up under the altar, I saw strange wires and fibers that seemed to be made of glass. "Awwwwesooooome" I almost said out loud when Malevolent, the leader of all priests and three others, bent before the altar doing homage to the crystal. They rose and peered into it, seeking my whereabouts as they did some sort of mind link together.

All they could see was the altar. They didn't know I was under it. Malevolent concluded, "He must be able to block the force's sensors. We'll have to find him the hard way." After a brief prayer, they left me alone tucked under the altar.

From the silence of their departure, I began to raise myself to peer out from my little space when one of the buckles on my pack must have touched against something in the underside of the altar for my movement created a series of short circuits, sparks and smoke. This so startled me that I jumped up and banged my shoulder against the overhang of the altar.

As I spun around, I snagged my pack's strap on one of the claws holding the crystal and tipped the crystal from the clutch of the golden three fingered hand. As I struggled to free myself, I panicked. I jerked real hard and I tilted the centerpiece of the altar. Unbeknown to me, the black crystal rolled from its place; across the altar and, as I struggle to free myself, the crystal rolled into

13

my pack that was half open because I was pulling so hard.

In my panic, all I could think of was getting out of there. I could hear the footsteps of the priests returning down the hall. I ran to the curtain beneath a high balcony, where, climbing up behind the curtain, I was able to perch upon a small ledge part way up the wall. I was behind the curtain and well-hidden from the eyes of any priests.

Even as I climbed, one of the priests cried, "The Holy Crystal is gone! The source has been stolen. Raise the alarm!" Unseen by the scurrying priests, I crawled out onto the ledge's extension and into a small passageway up high near the ceiling where I lay for some time completely concealed from view.

The ledge was invisible behind the upper ridge of the curtain. I relaxed. I must have fallen asleep because I awoke to the sound of many voices coming through an opening further along the ledge. I crawled over and peeked down into the next room.

It is strange that I can remember all this so many years ago, especially since they have finally captured me and I am being tortured on the rack. "Through the pain," the Elves had said, "put your mind through the pain." Suddenly my body is so filled with pain, I cannot remember. I cannot think. The pain, the pain, the pain is unbearable. "Ahhhhhhhhhhhh." And again, my mind goes black. From deep within the blackness of a world of pain, I am awakened.

And then the voice: "Remember," it soothes. "Embrace the pain. Every problem is caused by its solution." The voice so loving, as though it were the source of life itself. I see the eyes of Misty, my Elfin friend and Doray, my mentor. As my Elfin friends gather around me, my consciousness changes, as if from another dimension of time, my memory returns me to life. I am once again within the journey that brought me to this place when all hope was gone.

I remembered then, as though it were now, my mind taking me back to the Black Stone Monastery when I was awakened in the early hours of darkness by noises coming from the next room.

I crawled quietly, ever so quietly, to the end of the shaft, where I was hiding and peered down on hundreds of priests filing in processions carrying lighted candles.

The procession was almost magical, yet an ugly thing, a contrast of dark and light in motion, and yet a thing of beauty and pageantry. Hundreds of candles moved like ribbons of light twining into patterns and finally come to rest in a great bouquet of light. In the background was the most beautiful music I had ever heard, from an all-male choir standing on a special balcony across the hall from where I was hidden.

It was the Black Stone Monastery's finest hour, when the opposition was to be crushed and the only voice remaining to be heard would be "the word of God." I was witnessing the great judgment chamber, where inquisitional hearings were held and judgments pronounced and the "power of God" was manifest.

After prayers, the singing of hymns, and a Mass, Malevolent rose, dressed in a pure white robe, and raised his arms as he addressed the congregation and called the court of inquisition to order. All arose, as the lights went out and only the large torches at the center of the hall were left to throw their ominous shadows across the faces of a thousand worshipers.

As he started the proceedings, Malevolent walked in great majesty up the curving marble stairs to an elevated throne. It was made of what looked like solid white marble encrusted with gold, carefully cast into myriads of shapes, with angels, animals and humans all struggling in agony and yet all embossed in the finest of gems. Lights reflected in radiant splendor as it glittered in the night from its platform standing higher than any other in the room.

As Malevolent seated himself on the throne, it was then that Nicholas saw beside it a second seat, where the dwarf sat, totally dressed in black. Below them, but still above the others, sat a Council of Twelve in a perfect circle. Each priest was dressed in pure black. In the next circle, I counted 144 others who waited in an amphitheater that surrounded the council. Each section sat in an order that could be marked according to the degree of black in their robes. The lesser priests to the back of the hall were too numerous to count because they faded into the darkness of the great hall and showed mostly gray in their cloaks. The great torches from the center now vaguely lit the entire assembly.

"Brothers!" boomed Malevolent in a deep guttural roar. "Let your hearts be pure and your minds cleared of any ungodly thoughts." The silence was total. He waited a moment and then continued. "This inquisition is called by God to cleanse his church. Let no ungodly thought enter this room that we may be united against the workers of the Devil." Not a sound could be heard in the entire assembly. "When we bring in Satan's follower," he continued, "we must all be pure. Let us pray." A long chanting prayer followed. I lay there fascinated by the proceedings and momentarily lost to the danger of my own predicament.

At the end of the prayer, Malevolent nodded his head and a priest pulled a great ribbon of cloth that hung from ceiling to floor. Immediately a bell tolled and two great doors at one end of the assembly hall opened. Two priests held on firmly to the arms of a staggering man. It was, I could guess, the candidate to be submitted before the inquisitional tribunal for purging. Then, as he came closer to the light of the torches, I realized he was the man I had seen on the rack! He was the one who had been tortured!

From my perch, I watched, frozen in bewilderment at the drama that unfolded before me. Malevolent ordered a priest to read a long list of charges against the man. Another priest was called upon to read the man's "confession" as proof to the inquisition board that the man was a worshiper of Satan.

"You are charged with heresy and Satan worship" charged Malevolent. "You have sought to steal the power of God by making this satanic device. Did you not make this device?" A priest held up a kite, made of wood and cloth, and brought it forward. Not one of the priests would touch the kite so they extended it on two cross poles. As one the entire congregation grasped their silver crosses that hung about their necks and held them up between them and the kite.

The kite was thus brought forward and placed at the feet of the man. "Do you deny you made this?" Malevolent asked in a loud voice so all could hear. The man dropped his head. "Speak so all can hear!" commanded Malevolent. "By your own confession, you have admitted to your foul deeds."

The man remained silent. "God's will be done," spoke Malevolent. "By decree it is avowed that no device may be constructed which attempts to steal the power of God. This is an offense to God. His power can only be controlled through his church." He paused, allowing his words to sink into the congregation.

Then he continued, "This device floats. It flies in the air. It is therefore satanic." The crowd murmured its approval. "It is inspired by the great ruler of darkness who seeks devices such as this to deceive people. He makes them enjoyable and seemingly harmless." The crowd grew more restless in the rising tempo from the throne. It was if they responded mindlessly to match his emotions. "But the council of the Inquisition has uncovered the truth!" Louder murmurs of and some shouts of approval arose from the congregation.

"Any attempt to defy the natural order, where all physical things flow downward and all celestial things flow upward, is a violation of the laws of God. Only the followers of Satan would attempt such heresy. This man, by his own admittance, is such a heretic." Turning toward the man, he scowled, "Do you deny these charges?" The room suddenly became totally silent.

Weakly, at first, then in a voice growing with more confidence, the man replied, "I know that birds fly. Insects, seeds, clouds and even fish sometimes fly. Arrows fly and no one would be without arrows during these troubled times. I know in my moments of greatest joy in my love of life and of God, I jump towards the heavens and give thanks to my God for the life that is in me. In all things I honor my God. This device is but an inquiry into the joy of life and invention. It is a toy which delights children and gives them pleasure."

"Observe my brothers," cut in Malevolent, "how cleverly this man has twisted the truth. See how clever the followers of Satan are. To give children pleasure! Indeed it is the work of the devil. Children are born *to work!*" he shouted. "To serve their masters and create a better life for their elders!" The crowd murmured its approval. He waited. Then as the crowd quieted, he continued. "Such pernicious doctrines, such as to have children wile their time away in such frivolous activities seeking after the pleasures of the flesh, is one of Satan's devices!" he roared and the crowd cheered. "By his own words, he has condemned himself." Again the crowd cheered.

As they began to calm down, the man spoke. "If it is a sin," he said aloud, "to seek the happiness of others, I am guilty. If it is a sin to love children, then put me to death." He stood erect and proud. The crowd gasped and almost seemed to back up from the man. "I only pray, that in some future, God will grant children the freedom to explore possibilities, to play, to grow up loving life, and yes, I will say it...to enjoy playing with toys such as this."

A gasp escaped from the body of the priests. Then, into the almost audible silence that again hovered over the chamber, Malevolent spoke. "By his own mouth you have heard his heresy." He bowed his head and continued as if in great sorrow, "All our efforts to save him have failed. Even to purge him with pain has not weakened his resolve!" Then lifting his arms to heaven, he shouted: "We commend him to you Lord." He waited a moment and bowed his head. Then, as if in a magnanimous afterthought, his head rose and he asked, "Is there anyone in the audience who would defend this man?"

Silence. I was so stunned, I was immobile. Hidden from everyone and everything going on, I did not want to know such things. I did not want to be a part of any of this. I wanted my home and my father.

"All those in favor of the ultimate act of love, please indicate by raising your hand." The vote was unanimous. "You are pronounced guilty and unrepentant of blasphemy and heresy. You remain unrepentant and immovable in your satanic deceptions. It is out of our love and concern for your soul that we now pronounce: You shall receive no last rights and are hereby condemned to endless hell. You forfeit all your lands and wealth to the Church and your children and family shall be paupers and shall work in the sweatshops all the days of their lives."

The man pulled himself erect. "You condemn me only for the labor my family will benefit to you and this ungodly band of thugs you call priests!" He shouted. "You are not of God. You are of the dark side."

Before the man can say more, Malevolent nodded to a priest who pulled on a red curtain rope. A large door folded down in front of the altar. It opened onto a huge volcanic pit beneath the floor. "You are condemned to hell mortal. The great beast of Satan awaits your soul in the everlasting pit of fire and brimstone."

From my perch I could see plainly through the opening down into the pit. It was the most frightening thing I had ever seen. Great billowing flames shot into the air below the room. Their heat and light came roaring up into the room. The flames leapt toward the opening in the floor and the fumes from the pit below billowed across the audience. "This must truly be the pits of hell," I thought as I shrank back into the shadows of my hiding place.

Then, in the shadows of the pit below, a great Griff, a beast like a dragon, stalked the opening. It was larger than the Griff I had faced in the crypt! Much larger! Then, before I could even think about it, another rope was pulled. The man dropped with a soul-rending scream, out of sight, into the pit. I knew then the dragon of Satan, the great beast of the pits of hell, for his great head loomed up, close to the opening, and I knew that beast must have devoured him. Even as the thought began to register, a horrible roar, worse than thunder in the height of a mountain storm, filled the hall, overpowering everything. Even my own scream of protest was lost in the magnitude of the roar of the beast of hell.

In the midst of the chaos that followed, Malevolent's voice boomed through the chamber, "Cleanse your selves from all unholy thoughts!" he commanded as he stood before the thrown. "Men of righteousness have no thoughts but to follow God and his priesthood!" He sat down. A chant began, led by the priests of the Council of Twelve. "God is good, God is good." The congregation of priests began to chant in unison, "God is good, God is good." They repeated the chant over and over. "God is good. God is good."

I found upon myself the sweat of fear and had no control of my trembling. I had shriveled back, behind the corner nearer the curtain and I was gripped in the vice of what I had just witnessed. Then, from the upper part of the chamber, priests in gray appeared and began a beautiful song, in four-part harmony, giving praise to Jesus. It is beautiful music, the most beautiful I ever heard but it did not fit. It seemed so out of place in the gruesomeness of the inquisition I had just witnessed.

As if to answer my thoughts, the roar of the beast echoed through the hollow halls of the rock-hard monastery. The beast of Satan, the Griff, was raising its complaint from the pits of hell.

As the music ended, Malevolent stood. I heard his words echoing through my head; "The source crystal is missing. A boy – a Sender, has stolen it! Find him my brethren! Find him and restore the source to its altar or our order will end and God's work will have been dealt a terrible blow. Find the boy. Find the crystal. Spare no effort. Go! Now!" he commanded and every person filed out of the amphitheater.

It would only be a matter of time. I knew they would find me as soon as someone realized the ledge was large enough to conceal me. In spite of it all, I felt weary and sleepy. In the little indented shelf, as the priests combed the monastery, my last thoughts were of my father. Where was he? Was he still alive? Could he have survived the avalanche? I felt terribly alone as I curled up in my little hiding place. Finally, I must have gone to sleep.

Father had been digging in the snow. He discovered my hat and had worn his hands raw desperately scooping out a deepening tunnel into the ravine where he thought I must have been buried. He dug down about 20 feet when suddenly the snow began to shift. The sides of his tunnel began to cave and he desperately scrambled toward the surface. He was buried for awhile and barely was able to dig his way out again. He realized then, that there was no way he could recover my body without help. Nevertheless, he dug on and on, widening the tunnel, careful to get branches to fortify it. As it grew dark, his hands began to bleed. When he realized the blood was freezing and he could no longer feel anything, he rested and wept for me, his only son.

"Nicholas, Nicholas. You must not die. You must not die! Wait for me Nicholas! Hang on! Stay brave my son! I will go and get a shovel and tools!" He trudged on weary feet over the pass to his shop where he worked into the night to forge a big shovel.

The next thing I remember was being awakened by a noise. It was in the dead of the night and a large procession of priests was filing into the judgment chamber. Each held a lighted torch. Over 1000 men assembled, forming the order of a pyramid. At the top peak, looking down upon them from a great height, Malevolent addressed the group with gothic authority.

"What have you found, my Brothers?" One of the twelve stood. "We have searched the entire monastery and have not found the boy who is the Sender. All those in the sweatshop are accounted for and are securely held."

"This threatens the order!" growled Malevolent. He was clearly upset. "He has stolen the sacred crystal and is hiding somewhere in the monastery. Continue the search! Look in all the places you have looked and where you have not looked, look there."

The priests got no sleep that night. They filed out to continue what must have been the most massive search ever made of the monastery. They must have been everywhere. Finally, the dwarf entered the altar room. He himself began to search behind each hanging tapestry and curtain. He came closer and closer to where I was hiding; I could see him throwing each drape aside.

To avoid being discovered, I had to crawl silently back along the ledge until I reached the center of the crossing point between two walls. There was a small indentation there. When I pushed against it, I discovered it had a little give on its innermost side. The old plaster had cracked. It showed a square-indented frame that had been plastered over.

As quietly as I could, I pushed against it and it gave ever so little. It must have been a very old opening that had been covered over with a thin layer of plaster many years ago. There was no other way for me to go, so I pushed on the plaster as hard as I could. Suddenly, without any warning, I plunged forward into empty blackness and plummeted downward between the walls.

I remember careening off a wall and bouncing through a beam that cracked and disintegrated under my weight. It slowed my fall and I grabbed out with my hands just as I thudded into the next beam. It did not break but I lay a moment almost knocked out. But I held on as I listened to the debris from my fall as it plunged downward bouncing off the walls into what seemed to be as an endless pit of darkness. Finally I heard it hit the bottom.

Very carefully I swung myself up to sitting position on the beam. I could, for just a moment, make out what appeared to be a stone chute slanting downward against the inner wall. What little light was there was suddenly cut off. I looked up and could see far above me, the head of the dwarf peering down into the darkness below. The beam upon which I was perched started to give way so I had no choice but to quickly fling myself over toward the chute.

As I did so everything seemed to collapse. The beam gave way and I tumbled onto what seemed to be the chute. I kept rolling and dropping, tumbling, tumbling down, down, down the chute.

It must have been a laundry chute because when I came out of it I found myself smothered among a great pile of dirty black cloaks. I tore them away and, as I looked up, there, through the misty atmosphere, I saw great billows of steam rise from stoneware vats. Stirring the vats were children. I looked upon the scene as though it was frozen in time and imprinted in my memory forever.

I could clearly see the children were chained. My eyes roamed through the great cavern. There must have been more than 100 children in this immense cave. Some were carrying clothes and dumping them into vats. Others were filling or draining the large circular stone vats. Around some vats were children walking in endless circles, pulling a windlass that drove a gigantic water wheel. The wheel was attached to a series of ropes upon which a line of never-ending buckets were lifted from deep down in the pits of hell. I could see children everywhere. Slowly I came to the realization. "This is a sweat-shop!" I dropped back into the laundry shoot and hid. A whole new fear began to grip me.

My father had warned me about sweatshops where children were enslaved to do the work. They had arisen all over the country since the inquisitions had begun. This one must have been for the monastery. The children seemed half-dead and half-starved. All were chained. As I watched them, half hidden in the laundry basket, they seemed so listless. They moved like things from another world with the life drained almost completely out of them.

No one talked. There was no laughter, no play and no voices. I marveled how so many children and not one sound from any of them for my ears heard only the sounds of work.

I was preparing to get out of the laundry container when one of the boys on the windlass saw me. My eye caught his and we stared eye-to-eye for just a moment and something seemed to come alive in him. He looked quickly around, his eyes suddenly large and round. He raised his hand to his lips and signaled me to be quiet. Then, without seeming to do anything unnatural, he raised one finger and pointed. I followed the direction of his pointing finger and saw, lounging against the wall, a priest in black who held within his hand, a short whip. I could barely see him through the steam in the room rising from the vats.

I glanced back but the boy was on the other side of the windlass. When he circled back to my side, I mouthed, "Please help me." He shook his head negative. As he started to turn to the away side of the windlass I mouthed back, "How do I get out of here?"

He raised his hands and looked at the chains. I raised mine and he saw no chains. His eyes grew bigger. He walked slowly around to the other side of the windlass. He did not look toward me when he came back around but only toward the priest. Drawn by some slight change in the dynamics, the priest began to saunter down toward the windlass. I ducked under the cloaks.

When the priest was well beyond me, I looked carefully out from under the pile. My new friend was just coming around the windlass as he pointed to the empty bucket descending through a jagged cleft opening in the floor. As the great windlass turned, driven by the children endlessly walking in circles, buckets of warm water were lifted from the depths of the pit, emptied into the vat, and then the buckets descended once again into the pit.

"He wants me to get into the bucket and go into the pit!" I said to myself. "I don't want to go into the pit. That's where the beasts are and the hell fire!" I raised my head and shook it; "No."

The priest turned back and slowly made his way back to his watch position against the wall. I was thinking all the while. "I can't stay here. I can't go anywhere in this place that the priests won't catch me. They would throw me in the pit anyway or put me on the rack, maybe the pits of

20

hell are no worse than these pits. OK. At least it can't be any worse than the crypts and I survived that." This was the way my mind was working. Finally, I raised my head.

The boy was pointing to the empty bucket. I nodded "Yes." He immediately signaled me, "Now!" I took a quick look at the priest and scampered over just as the bucket was going into the crack in the floor. I jumped in and gave a look to my friend that said, "I hope you are right." I whispered, "If I can help you I will." Only then did the boy smile.

Chapter Three

The Griffs in the Pitts of Hell

I disappeared into the darkness. Down, down, down I went until I began to see strange shadows moving across the walls of the great crack into which I was descending. The light grew brighter and then, all at once, I knew it was light from the fires of hell. I know now it was an active volcano but then, when I was six, it was the fires of hell and as scary as anything a boy could face. I looked down into the darkness, shivering from fear. Gradually I began to realize I was being lowered into a pool of steaming, pitch black water.

When the bucket hit the water, before I could do anything, I sank right to the bottom. I found myself on my back. I couldn't roll over. I did not realize it but the crystal in my pack weighed me down and held me on my back. I struggled desperately, clawing at the water. I screamed my panic and found myself choking and my lungs filling with water. I remember trying to wriggle out of the backpack but it was no use, I was passing out, glued hopelessly and helplessly to the bottom of the pool by the weight on my back.

As my mind clouded over, I felt something brushing past my arm. Instinctively, my hand grabbed out in a last act of life and I felt something solid. I held on for all I was worth and was lifted by the bucket on the rotating windlass, upward through the water.

I barely broke the surface and gasped a couple of gulps of life-saving air, when I realized I was being lifted back up into the sweatshop. Far above me I could see the crack through the volcanic floor. Down below, the pool was beginning to fall away from under me. I didn't want to go where the priests imprison children and put them in sweatshops. I saw the shore below and thrust myself toward it as I let go of my life-saving bucket.

This time I hit the water feet first. As the weight of the pack began to drag me over onto my back, I fought to regain control as I sank to the bottom. This time I landed on my hands and feet. I crabbed along the bottom and getting desperate for a breath, I scrambled up the embankment into the air. I clawed myself onto the black sand beach. Gasping great breaths and still half choking on the water I had swallowed, I collapsed, draining water from my mouth and nose.

I opened my eyes to the mysterious light from the volcanic fire way down in the great cave of hell. Shadowy forms cast themselves about the walls and ceiling. I looked slowly around without moving. Strange noises, of steam rising, boiling and bubbling, echoed through the chamber like some ancient orchestra playing off-key notes.

Finally, I pulled myself to my knees and looked around the cave. I knew I had to get out of there. Way up on the wall appeared a ledge, which I thought I might be able to use in my escape.

It appeared to lead to a crevice from which a feint light glowed. I stood up.

Looking for a way to get to the ledge, I spotted what appeared to be a large rock formation that angled upward almost to the ledge. "If I can get to the very top, I might be able to find a way to climb the rest of the way," I thought to myself as I started up the incline. As I climbed, I did not notice the strangeness of the rock, nor the spike-like outcroppings that made the climbing a lot easier. I was just anxious to get to the top and get out of this terrible pit.

As I neared the uppermost part where the rock seemed to narrow and the outcroppings became more evident, the whole mountain seemed to move beneath me. Instinctively, I grabbed onto the shaft of rock between two rows of outcroppings. I found myself being lifted upward instead of falling downward. Below me I could see a gigantic body getting to its feet. I screamed when I realized I was on the neck of the huge Griff - the mother of all Griffs – the Beast of Satan!"

It was three times the size of the creature in the water and, when it roared, the very fabric of what I was holding onto vibrated so loud that I almost lost my grip. Back and forth it whipped me, trying to rid itself of me. I hung on for dear life.

Turning its head, the Griff could see me but it could not reach me with its teeth because I was up too far on the back of its neck. It beat its mutant wings and roared again, trying to flip me off. It stamped its feet in frustration, waved its head back and forth and then it plunged its head and neck into the water.

My father had taught me how to hang on. I used to ride his back pretending he was a wild horse and he would buck and buck, trying everything to get me off. I was a pretty good rider and I needed it now. The Griff shook its head back and forth in the water but, because it had a double row of scales and I was in between them, it could not dislodge me so easily although it almost did.

Finally, it pulled its head from the water and rubbed its neck along the sand. My arms and feet were exposed and it burned and almost crushed my left elbow. I let go of my hold. I was thrown tumbling onto the black sand beach.

It was then that I first knew I had the black crystal. The impact knocked the crystal and my twirly out of my pack. As I came up out of the sand, I grabbed my twirly and rolled into a cleft between two rocks. It was barely big enough for me and the Griff was coming right on me, pressing me hard, with its head crashing into the cleft. The rocks stopped it. Its breath was so bad it almost suffocated me, so I pulled up my twirly and gave it a spin just as the Griff opened its mouth to roar at me.

The sparks lit the Griff's breath like lightning striking a tree. Flames shot down its mouth, then right down into its belly. It roared its pain and anger, and flames shot into the air. No longer did it care about me. It plunged itself into the water, the flames reaching each of its stomachs with a series of burping eruptions.

I heard a great commotion from around the cave as the roars of the mother Griff awakened the other Griffs. They began to bob and weave their heads back and forth and move toward me alarmed at the roars of the mother Griff. I was trapped. I knew I wouldn't last long and was desperately looking for a way out when I spotted the black crystal on the sand.

Subtle chimes resounded in my head and, before I knew what I was really doing, I scurried and picked up that crystal just as the Griff came full out of the water and thrust its head straight at me.

This was the first time I had actually touched the crystal and, before I knew what was happening, a stream of energy flowed through me and out of it. It surged through the Griff, stopping it in its tracks. I saw the energy flow into the water, across the black beach sand and all along the walls of the cave. It surrounded every Griff and coursed through them like hot milk on a cold winter's night.

It materialized out of the air around me and streamed through my body in waves of little life sparklets. In rainbows of color, energy cascaded from my body into the crystal and into the air, the water, the rocks and the Griffs. The crystal turned from black to clear white light. Then a great stream of energy jumped from the crystal to the Griff. A great cry was heard from throughout the cavern.

I looked up and could not believe what I saw. Myriads of shadowy human figures appeared from within the fire of the volcano! They were also coming out of the walls of the cave. Intuitively I knew at once that they were the lost souls of hell, caught forever in the Grid of Agony. They cried out for deliverance, gathering in great numbers around me, repeating over and over: "Sender, Sender, save us; save us from this terrible pit."

I was too shocked to do anything but just stand there, letting everything happen. Suddenly my attention was riveted on the Griff. Our eyes locked. Pulsating with the energy from the crystal as it surged around us and consumed us in its light, the dragon's flames and fury were turned aside. The crystal embraced and devoured the anger of the Beast of Hell!

Within the energy I could see shadows of strange things I could not begin to understand, of worlds of dwarfs, of great planets and civilizations from other times where galactic battles were being fought with so many great ships in the sky that I could not count them all. A huge black hole in space emerged and, as though I was able to travel through it, many life forms appeared. Suddenly before me in the air was the image of a wonderful starship manned by Elves giving commands and interposing the light into the darkness. I sensed the dark side of Elfin worlds and there I saw the dwarf and his great armadas. The dominion of the black dwarfs was locked in battle with Elfin worlds. Back and forth the battle raged. Immense energies interchanged between them and entire galaxies collapsed.

Drawn by the noise, the priests of the monastery had discovered where I was and they began to enter the cave along the upper ledge carrying torches. Hundreds of them began filing in. I was so taken by the light and energy of the crystal and by my experience with the Griff, I hardly noticed the life and death struggle the seven other Griffs were having. They must have risen from other parts of the cave. Now, together, they had placed themselves between the priests and me. But the priests begin to drive them back with spears and torches and the Griffs fought back, roaring and snapping at them.

There were too many priests. Using their torches, they were driving the Griffs back so they could get to me. I suddenly realized I was being surrounded.

But the leader of the Griffs, frozen in mind lock suddenly broke into conversation. Within my mind I heard the words; "You are the Sender?" It was both a question and an answer.

"How can I hear you?" I wanted to know. "Am I really talking to you?"

"Oh yes. Only a Sender could talk with me!" The Griff sounded amazed. "But I don't even know what a Sender is!" I cried, now quite distressed by the approach of the priests. "A Sender? Oh yes, please forgive me. What is a Sender? Ah, yes. Well, a Sender is someone who can send love out and it is felt everywhere." She had said this as though everyone would naturally understand it.

I still didn't get it and noticing my concerned glances at the onslaught of the priests, she continued, "The love of a Sender has the power to transform evil. Evil cannot resist because you know the potential of every evil is good." She was talking about the power of good to do something and I didn't really want to talk about good and evil. I wanted to get out of there but I also sensed the beast was trying to tell me something, so I swallowed my fear and listened.

"Evil is a reversal or trapping of life energy so it cannot be released to fulfill its potential. All these souls trapped in hell are awaiting an opportunity to be freed to fulfill their potential. When you touch their source, their life energy is released. They are transformed. Ah. If only I could be a Sender, I could get out of here. I could fly forever."

The priests, drawing nearer and nearer, battled all around me. Even above the shouts, the roaring flames, the spears and the Herculean efforts of the Griffs, I could hear the Griff clearly: "We have been imprisoned here for hundreds of years." A priest almost grabbed me but I slipped under the legs of the Griff and she whipped the Priest with her tail sending him into the water. "We have but one desire. To fly free! To fly and fly and fly! Ohhh! To be a Sender! We could get out of here!"

Suddenly I realized: "If you were a Sender, you could get out of here? You could?"

"Of course," she bobbed her great head up and down. "How?" I screamed over the noise. "Why," she screamed back above the noise of the battle, "through the portal under the water. Then I would be able to fly and I could just go through walls."

I looked into the water. The morning sunlight could be seen reflecting through a small opening under the water. Just then about 100 priests attacked with their torches. The Griffs were

27

driven to the very edge of the water.

"Go," said the Griff. "We will be all right. Go. Save yourself. This world could use a Sender."

"You want to fly?" I asked. I couldn't just leave them alone like this. The great Griffs were fighting valiantly by my side. But my moments were short.

"We all want to fly. We all want to serve the love force of life. But we are trapped as guardians of the Grid of Agony and the lost souls in the spirit prison of hell." She bowed her head and swung it into a wall of priests.

I barely had time to grasp what was being said. I could see that she and the others were weaving back and forth, holding the Priests at bay. I wanted to stay and, for a moment, I wavered. It was at that moment the dwarf appeared.

"Go. Now," retorted the Griffs in unison. Just as the dwarf shot a bolt of dark energy from its hands, I jumped into the water. I could feel the bolt penetrate the water but, since I still held the crystal, somehow its light energy protected me. Even under water I could feel the power of the darkness as it closed around me. As I scrambled along the bottom, I tried to make my way toward what I knew must be the opening. I wondered how I was possibly going to make it when suddenly I felt a great pushing force from behind me. I could not turn my head to look but, in retrospect, I think now that it must have been the Griff.

Then, as I was running out of air and my lungs began to ache, the darkness suddenly opened before me and, through the little opening, I was squeezed through from some force behind me. Out into the fresh air I plunged. I gasped for breath as I felt my feet sink into the warm wet mud of the bottom of the pond. I had escaped!

Still clinging to the crystal, I climbed from the warm water and found myself in a secluded cove. I turned around and saw, rising straight above me, the almost vertical cliffs of the mountain. High above, built upon the top of the mountain cleft, loomed the great black stone walls of the monastery, reaching out of sight into the sky.

Finally, I stood on solid ground, out of the pond and out of the monastery! I was free at last! I put the crystal down carefully in fresh snow and began to wring some of the water out of my clothes. I spaced my jacket, sweater and shirt out on some bushes to let them dry a little in the warm sun. It beat down from the walls and reflected off the pool to make this an extra warm area. Grass and shrubs poked their heads up through the partly melted snow. Beside the spring, the tracks of deer and other small animals could be seen in the snow and in the mud. I replaced the crystal carefully in my back pack, anxious to return to my father, wondering if he was still alive. Determined to get home, I put on my partly dried clothes and struck off immediately for our valley.

On the way, I couldn't forget the Griffs. "They are people, too," I kept saying to myself, as

I wove my way among the trees, across the crusted snow, over the crest and into our private little valley. "They are different than I, but they are people just the same." I worried about the lost souls encased within the pits. I could not fathom any solution so I began to think only of getting home, the only home I knew. Would my father be there? Was he still alive? I made my way as quickly as I could down through the trees across the meadow. Then I heard the sound of metal banging on metal. The sound was coming from my father's smithy shop.

---

* The legend of Santa has existed in many cultures for centuries before the European cultures adopted it into their folklore in the late 16th century.

Chapter Four

My Father's Workshop

Quietly I crept up and looked in. It was a habit of mine never to interrupt my father when he was working on something. So I just quietly peered around the corner. My father was working with such intensity, he did not notice me. He seemed to be making a shovel, for he was pounding out a shape that could only be for snow.

I looked around, standing perfectly still. I noticed, on a bench nearby, a circular silver fan that opened like an umbrella. For just a moment I felt such a deep appreciation for my father. He had worked steadily in his smithy shop ever since I could remember. Now all the tools and toys of his own making surrounded him.

I came out of my moment of reverie when I realized he must have been anxious over the loss of me. I saw then how he drove himself feverishly in his work to make the shovel.

Without a sound, I took off my backpack. As I did so, the crystal rolled out. Without really thinking, I took the crystal in my hands. Suddenly wanting to surprise him, I gently rolled the crystal between his firmly placed feet. Hearing the sound, he looked down and there, in the crystal, he could see my face reflected in its mirrored surface.

"Nicholas?" he asked, peering at the crystal. I laughed as my father said, "Nicholas, do not play with me. Come out of that rock."

"But I am here father," I giggled, "behind you." My father turned and with a cry of joy he took me up in his arms. He danced, shouted and sang praises to the Lord. He wept; we both wept. He was so joyous to see me and I to see him that we were both overwhelmed.

"I thought I'd lost you," he cried. "Oh Nicholas, I thought I had lost you." The love between us was overpowering. "I thought I had lost you, too, Father and that I might have to go work in a sweatshop!" I replied. "There were spiders and bugs and dragons and dwarfs and giants Daddy. There were the pits, the fire of hell and there were..."

"Yes, yes Nicholas," he cut in. "I, too, had my nightmares. But it is over now. Now let's see how you look."

"But Daddy, I was in the pit!" I exclaimed. "It was the pit of hell and the beast of Satan was there!"

"Nicholas." He raised his eyebrows.

"And the priests … they torture people and put them to death." I stopped.

Unbeknown to my father or me, the black crystal, lying at our feet suddenly seemed to come to life. Out of its inner depths of darkness emerged a large, almost completely black eye. The eye was open and, with careful scrutiny, one might recognize it as belonging to a certain dwarf. The eye began to rotate as if looking around, trying to locate a point of reference.

In clearing a space on his workbench, my father swept a pile of old canvas down onto the floor. Although I didn't notice it at the time, that single act probably saved our lives. The canvas covered the crystal and blocked Dwarg's view. His eye into our privacy was closed.

Father sat me up on the bench. "Now let's see if you are all right. How in the world did you get out of the avalanche?" He began to look me over. "I climbed up through the sewer pipe," I explained. "Father, there were bugs and dragons and dwarfs and giants and . . ."

"Yes, yes, son. I had my nightmares too." He did not want to talk about what he thought were my nightmares.

"But..." I stammered. He cut me off. "No buts now," he said. "Through a sewer pipe, you say? Then you must have a bath. We shall go immediately to the stream and wash this smell off."

"But..." Again, he cut me off. "No buts, besides I need to finish a surprise I have for you and I don't want you around for the next little while, he said. "Let's get you cleaned up so I can finish my surprise."

"A surprise? But..." I was interested but I just had to tell him about the Griffs. "Was that another but?" he challenged.

"Oh, OK," I replied, "But I have to tell you about the dragons." It never occurred to me that I might never have the chance to tell him. We had always been together.

"It's a deal," he said. "Let's go get you cleaned up." He swept me off the bench as he grabbed a bucket, some soap and a towel.

I shivered through a meticulous scrubbing in the cold, clear stream water, looking all the while at my father's hands. I donned a clean set of clothing and warm boots. "Father, what happened to your hands?" I asked.

"It is nothing. I got it digging out of the snow," he whispered. I continued, "But they must hurt." Then he told me something I would never forget and that, years later, saved my life: "Pain is in the mind. Having you back is such a joy to me that my pain is transformed by my joy."

At the time it did not sink in. "But..." was all I could muster.

He looked at me with one eyebrow raised. He was about to talk about all my "buts" but then he kindly explained; "Nicholas, my son, such pain as this is only the icing on the cake of love, so I have no thought of the pain only my joy at having you back. Mind you, the pain might come back if I don't finish my new birthday gift for you."

"What is it Father?" I sensed he wanted to focus on something else. "Oh, please tell me. What is it?"

"No, you must wait," he teased. I talked my father into letting me scrub my clothes because I knew his hands were in such bad shape. After I washed and rinsed them the way Father would do, I hung the clothes on a wooden pole that he had made especially for hanging cloths. I went into his shop but he waved me away with a wink of his eye and a "Ho, ho! We wouldn't want to spoil the surprise!"

"Go play by the stream and don't come back until later this afternoon. Your birthday surprise must be completed before dark. As you know," he chided me, "the present must be delivered before the end of the day." As I turned to leave, I heard him mumble to himself, "And before my hands stiffen."

I wanted so much to tell him about the monastery but it would have to wait. A birthday gift must always be delivered on the evening before the birth and I was excited to know what he was making for me. I wandered off down the stream, picking my way among the stones.

"AHHHHHHHH!" Pain. There is nothing but pain. Back on the rack! The giant Benton and the dwarf Dwarg enjoyed stretching me. They delight in taunting me while torturing me. It is the same room in which the man was tortured years before.

The chamber now has two racks for stretching people as well as an iron maiden, head shrinker, knuckle cruncher and the various tools of the torture-to-truth trade. All are designed as a confrontation of pain. My pain is becoming unbearable. I am about to scream when the almond eyes of the Elf Misty return to my mind. "Focus." I can hear her voice. "Focus your mind, Nicholas," she reminds me. "Remember."

Doray, commander of the Starship, stands before the holoscan screen. "They still have him on the rack. We have very little time. Mefa, what is happening to the grid?" "We are impacting in three minutes, Captain." "Tedo, report. Do we have permission from the Intergalactic Council?"

"We do, Captain. Permission granted. We may proceed," comes his response.

"Do it now!" the captain commands.

Then the face of my father appears.

"Pain is in the mind, Nicholas. Remember, when I told you that having you back was such a joy to me that my pain was transformed by my joy? Remember that pain is sensitivity that has nowhere to go," he gently reminds me. I can hear him and my mind goes back to that fateful day when three things happened, all at that same moment in time.

And those three things changed the history of the world and the galaxy.

While I went to play along the stream, my father had picked up the puffer. It was an invention of his, a fan-shaped umbrella, designed to collapse and open according to wind pressure so it formed into a toy parachute. He attached it to an arrow that he screwed into the inside center, much like an umbrella handle. He stepped out of his toy shop into the yard of our small farm and looked around to make sure I wasn't looking.

Our farm was nestled in a wooded valley, isolated from the town and the monastery. It was a peaceful and beautiful place, a place of refuge from the suffering of the cities and towns. He went to the corner of the shop and peeked around, checking to make sure that I was well away and not able to see what he is doing. Then he put the arrow into a bow, drew back and shot it into the air.

At that same moment, a priest, dressed in black, was walking briskly along the road high above our farm on his way to the Black Stone Monastery. At one point the road rose above the ridge where a traveler could look down upon our home. As the Priest paused to rest, he looked down into the valley and saw my father come out of the shop, draw the bow back and shoot the arrow.

The priest's eye, drawn to the movement of the archer's draw, watched the arrow fly upward. He looked to see what the man was shooting at but there was nothing there. Then, to his astonishment, the arrow opened with a puff and began is slow decent, floating toward the ground.

The Priest's eyes widened in amazement and he instinctively threw one arm up to cover his face as he drew his silver cross from the chain around his neck.

Keeping the cross between him and the "satanic" device, he stepped into the shadows so he could not be seen and raised his hood to cover his head. With fear-filled eyes and shaking limbs, he faded silently into the shadows of the woods. After a moment of prayer and meditation to strengthen his resolve, he began working his way down the hill toward our farm. Keeping almost invisible in the forest, he melted into the shadows. Holding the cross before him, he neared the edge of the woods where he could view father and the shop more closely.

My father, seeing that the puffer worked, was so delighted. "Ho! Ho! Ho!" he chortled to himself as he skipped across the yard to catch the slowly descending arrow. At 35 years of age, my father was one of the world's first toy makers. He returned to his shop, taking a quick look in the direction across the meadow to see the stream where I was playing.

"Ho, ho, ho," he chucked, pleased with himself.

In his shop, toys and inventions of all kinds surrounded him. All were of his own making. He had a propeller, double twisted with a square hole in the center. It fit upon a tightly twisted, square-sided silver rod about one meter in length. Under the propeller was a little ring. When I pulled the ring along the rod, it forced the propeller upward and began to twirl so fast that the propeller would shoot off into the air, floating a great distance as a "twirler."

Father made me a flying discus from paper-thin silver. It was for hand throwing and would fly clear across the meadow. A toy boat with a broadcloth sail lay on one bench next to the door. I had bent the tiller and it needed to be fixed. Its little sails rustled when the slightest breeze floated across it. It was just a little boat, about a foot high. There were three kites, all kinds of different gliders and a drawing of our (now lost) brightly colored red sleigh, with its curled front and hand-crafted sides and just enough sitting space to hold two people. The drawing still lay on the shop table.

The shop had a hayloft that was a warm and wonderful place to play while my father worked. I also begged my father to let me use his handcrafted tools, which he did from time to time, teaching me the art and science of toy making. I would resign to the hayloft and work on some toy until I would take it to him. He would give me a hint here and there and, like magic, a toy would soon appear.

His favorite work was the silver musketeer that stood upon a pillar of glass that was in a long tube of glass. My father had to blow the glass several times but finally got the musketeer standing just right, with its sword drawn, pointing forward. Then, running a silver wire from the hat of the musketeer up through the top of the glass tube, he connected it into the highest tree next to the shop. Leaving about the length of my finger between the end of the sword and the outside of the tube, he ran another silver wire down into a pool of water in the ground. We would wait until a big summer storm would come and then sit for hours waiting for the lightning to strike.

Strike it would, with a great burst of energy that would run down the wire, through the musketeer and out the end of his sword and jumping through the air to the wire and down into the ground. I would squeal with delight when it happened and he would laugh his jolly "Ho! Ho! Ho!"

On this day he set aside the silver parachute "puffer" and turned to a molding. Choosing a fine needle tool and wincing at his tender fingers, he began to carve the inside of the mold. He was working on the carving of a belt buckle, which he had almost finished so that it could be poured in silver.

His workbench always fascinated me. There were so many differently shaped carving tools. There was also a little carousel with dancing children made out of silver. He called it my Music Toy. He would set it in motion and I would sit enthralled as the chimes played a gentle little tune as the little carved people danced up and down. Several dolls, imaginary children for me to play with, were always strewn about. Wooden carts and the beginnings of various toys could be seen everywhere. He was always working on about 10 toys at once.

Through the beams of the clear afternoon sunlight, with floating specks of dust milling lazily around him, he looked upon the mold for my belt buckle. He turned it gently in his hands, lovingly caressing it. Picking a very fine tool from a wooden spindle shaft, he carved the finishing touches into the mold of the buckle.

At the top of the buckle he had imprinted the word "Santa" in Roman letters and on the bottom he carved eight tiny reindeer pulling a sleigh. He always hummed as he worked.

Off to the side of the meadow, beneath the towering trees, at a clear running stream that meanders among the 100 foot pines, I had been playing, waiting for the time to pass so my father could finish his surprise for me. I was anxious to tell him of my adventure in the monastery. The mountain water was so cool and clean.

At that same moment as my father shot the arrow, I had worked my way up the stream, as little boys will do, until I came to a place where I heard the chimes. They were so subtle that one could hardly notice. I looked in their direction and that is when my eyes fell upon a footprint in the mud at the side of the stream.

I stared at it. It was smaller than mine! But there were no children in our valley! "Whose could it be?" I asked myself.

Being lonely for other children, it roused my curiosity, and I began to explore in the direction of the footprint. I guess I must have followed the openings in the woods for a long way because I went up over the back ridge, deeper and deeper into the forest. I had never been that far before.

"Ahhhhhhhh! The pain. It is too much." Again the eyes of Misty appear. Her words, *"Remember, Nicholas. Remember."* In the background I can hear the voices of the Elves.

"We are monitoring him. He's still OK. He will only last three or four more minutes and then we will lose him to the Grid of Agony. Hurry, we must impact that grid within the next three minutes. We must begin the 'Relive' immediately, Captain." It was Doray.

"I hear you but the retractor is being monitored by the Delovian dark crystal. One more minute. Hang on, Nicholas. We must have the exact frequency combinations. The Delovians have constructed the Grid of Agony with great skill. People everywhere are programmed into it. We don't want to lose you again. Mefa? ... *"OK, Captain. Begin.... NOW."*

Then Comcom's voice peals out. *"OK, he's onto it. First sequence choice is to empower potential solution. He's coming toward the cave."* The Elves cheer.

Father, deeply involved in his shop, poured the molten silver into the mold while, unbeknown to him, the priest who had seen the puffer, made his way down to the workshop. He snuck up behind the building and was now watching Father's every action through the cracks in the wooden walls. As Father broke the mold away from the silver buckle, he was pleased. "It is a beauty," he said to himself. He began to touch it up, readying it to fit into a new black leather belt just for me.

The priest's eyes widened even more as he observed other toys -- carved images made of silver and paper and wood -- of birds and various folded papers folded to float. All the while he held desperately to his cross, keeping it before him in his trembling fingers, giving him courage. At last, satisfied he had seen enough and trembling with fear, he backed silently away and disappeared into the woods.

As he scurried through the shadows, returning the way he came, he mumbled to himself, "It is the work of the Devil himself. Indeed, to make such evil things! To try to steal the power of God! Ugh. Why, Lord? Why is there such evil in this world? Why can't things be the way you made them? Why do people have to mess things up?" He began to run as he reached to summit of the hillcrest between our valley and the monastery. Even in flight he mumbled, "This must be the greatest workshop of evil ever, trying to destroy the work of God! Huh! We shall see. We shall see."

As my father finished the belt and buckle, the priests of the Black Stone Monastery were gathering to hear the report from the exhausted Priest. At the same time, I was following the almost invisible trail of the little footsteps through the most magical of forests. All around me, the trees reached into the sky for more than 100 feet and great colonies of green moss grew around the trunks and on the branches. Giant ferns stood at attention, covering the floor of the forest in a carpet of every shade of green imaginable.

From time to time, a bouquet of brightly colored flowers would rise out of the green as though planted especially for its beauty. My father said that the birds and ants plant the flowers and tend them, too, in exchange for some of their nectar. He thought of the whole forest as a living being and said that if you love it, it will love you back. I loved the forest and always felt safe there but I didn't know about that love stuff.

I tracked among the great trees and through the giant ferns and over moss covered rocks not yet touched by the high snows. No sooner would I begin to lose the trail when I would find another footprint or sense a presence of the chimes that subtly led me further and further until finally I rounded a bend. There before me was the mouth of a huge cave.

Tucked under the crest of the next mountain valley, it lay hidden in shadows. As I drew nearer, the opening to the cave appeared larger and larger. Overpowered by its size and the depth of its shadows, I was a little scared. But I saw the little footsteps going into the cave. So, gradually, I made my way into the monstrous mouth of its inner chamber. Slowly my eyes grew accustomed to the dark. The cavern was huge inside, an awesome and mysterious place. Not far inside, around a corner, I could see a pulsating light. I found myself wondering what would make that kind of light.

My Father's Workshop

Chapter Five

The Starship

𝔐y father picked up a piece of cashmere wool cloth. He considered several dyes in a series of wooden corked bottles and set aside a bright red dye. "At least I will be able to find him in the snow," he chuckled to himself. He began to fashion a coat for me from the warm thick wool.

As my father was fashioning my winter coat, I tiptoed my way toward the pulsating light around the bend in the great cave. As I made my way around the bend, an incredible sight met my eyes.

There, in the middle of the cave, floating in the air, was a shimmering silver discus, a starship, bigger than a house. It floated more than 15 feet above the ground and was crowned with myriads of tiny lights and twirling colors, which blended in and out of its almost transparent, opal-like surface.

From the roof of the cave hung ancient vines and roots intertwined with rock cones like draped cloth. Everywhere the cave walls were covered with crystals. Huge quartz, emerald and topaz crystals reflected rainbows upon rainbows of light in a subtle, pastel panorama of beauty I had never witnessed before. Great roots ran down the walls in contrast to the soft light reflecting from the crystals. It was an ancient place. And right in the middle of the roof of the cave, a light beamed through a hole in the ceiling and cast itself upon the center of the inner chamber just beneath the starship.

My eyes roved the room until they centered beneath the Starship. There a great pastel crystal of light pulsated with life. It was, as I learned later, a double dodecahedron luminescent crystal. By taking in sunlight, it was able to order the light and reflect it up to fusion cells upon the underside of the starship. As I learned later, this living crystal used sunlight to fuel the ship. Then, beneath the ship, I spotted four little people! "Elves," as I soon discovered, were "tending" to the crystal and "feeding" the cells of the starship. Energy poured from the crystal into the cells on the bottom of the ship.

Never had I seen such a toy. The Elves were so intent upon their work, they did not notice me. All of them seemed totally preoccupied with their tasks. It was a strange and fascinating sight. I had never imagined anything like it was possible.

My mind flashed back to my father's workshop where the discus lay on a shelf. I saw in my mind's eye how I could throw the silver discus and how it could catch in the wind and stand suspended in the air. "Why, it's just like the discus! Amazing!" I murmured.

I was about to step closer when a shadow suddenly crossed the top of the cave, cutting off the sunlight. The energy flow from the crystal to the starship dematerialized as a ball of darkness bounced from the top of the starship, covering the crystal beneath it. It created a tilting action for the entire ship, which shuttered and started gyrating radically. The Elves jumped back. They gasped, shouting strange gibberish and, as the starship wavered back and forth, the shadow deepened until one edge of the ship touched the crystal!

A great explosion of energy threw me backward to the ground. When I looked up, the Elves in the middle of the smoke and confusion were kneeling in unison. Putting their right knee to the ground, they held their right wrists with their left hands while they focused their entire energy upon their wildly gyrating starship. It was beginning to swivel closer and closer to the walls of the cave. Energy streams poured from their wrists from some sort of crystal wristbands. As their energy beams surrounded the ship, it careened off several huge stalactites, creating great explosions of sound and debris. Finally, the Elves brought it under control.

When they finally got the Starship stable, it settled quietly onto some wooden braces, which seemed to materialize out of nowhere. A portal opened on the underside of the starship. Two more Elves came out of the ship, shaken and a little wobbly, but when they looked at the crystal, they were mortified. The great crystal has cracked.

"They are counteracting, Captain," reports Mefa. "They have fractured the tractor beam. We are locked into three-dimensional, unreal spacetime."

"Countermove. What are our options?" Comcom responds.

"All we can do is grow a new crystal. It will take years of earth time," he bows his head. Mefa seems the most concerned. "They have us trapped! They will monitor all of our moves now. It is possible that, we, ourselves, could get caught in that grid."

"Yes," replies Misty. "We are anchored into earth time and vulnerable in this dimension." Then, in the middle of the oppressive field they had just encountered, Comcom muses, *"Every problem is caused by its solution. There must be some solution causing this problem. Let's find out what it is. Keep monitoring the situation and let's see what we can do with that love frequency."*

Misty sums it up. "The Grid of Agony has been impacted by the love of human Senders before in history. See if we can help it along but, above all, we must do something to that grid. Its growth could signal the Black Hole and draw it toward the galaxy."

Using their star-crystal levitators strapped to their wrists, the Elves combined their efforts to lift their starship. To me, it appeared as magic. The Starship slowly moved up and I could see they were using the crystals on their wrists to lift the ship.

"Radical. Those could pull the sleigh up the mountain!" I thought to myself.

The Elves lifted one end of their scarred and scraped Starship first, further propping it up with some form of holographic support frame and then lifted the other end and also propped it up. Two of the Elves shuffled under the ship and brought pieces of the crystal out. It was one of the Elves who lifted her head to one side.

Large, almond-shaped eyes etched with ageless wisdom, set in the graceful lines of a face of total grace, turned on me. It was as though her sight was a secondary thing, for her eyes looked through and beyond me. As though, by some extra-sensory compassion, she was sensing an ancient knowing of me. The smile she gave me in the light of her recognition could have only come from years of loving experience. Like an ageless grandmother, forever young, she sensed something deeply about me and slowly turned to face directly into my being.

Without shifting her gaze or saying a word, she somehow signaled the others, for they turned as a group and looked right at me. For a moment time hung suspended in a chandelier of stillness, as though awaiting some void of potential to take form.

I was the first to move. I pulled myself erect and stood my ground. "After all," I said to myself, "they are smaller than me." "Hi," I said, waving my hand a little.

As a body, the Elves approached in a shuffling walk. Curious, exploring, they surrounded me. One of them stepped forward. He was obviously the captain. He talked in a strange gibberish until another interrupted and, with great gentleness, signaled that he wanted to touch my forehead with his finger. I looked at his hand, three-fingered with fingernails that were almost like claws, and I remembered the claw hand that held the dark crystal in the monastery.

He could see the doubt come into my eyes. But he was so kind and gentle, one look at his eyes and I knew it was OK. "Yeah. OK. Whatever." I nodded my head toward him.

As the Elf placed his middle finger upon my forehead, I felt better, calmed by his touch. Then, looking deeply into my eyes he began to talk gibberish. As he talked, sounds and clicks blurted in and out of my inner hearing. It was all without meaning. In a few seconds the words tuned in and he said, "Ah, there we are. We can talk now. My name is Comcom. What is your name?"

I said, "My name is Nicholas." The others introduced themselves.

"I am Doray," said one as he bowed a little. Then he turned to the one standing next to him and said, "This is Mefa." The other bowed as well. Then another spoke up. "I am Solah," said a third. Finally, the fourth Elf said, "And I am Tedo and this beautiful being is Misty." The sixth Elf nodded her head and I noticed she never took her eyes off me. I didn't know what else to do so, I said, "Glad to meet ya. Did you break your toy?"

The Elves looked at each other. "Toy?" Comcom asked. I turned my gaze upon the Starship. "Oh, yes! Our toy - it is ASTAR, our starship."

"Would you like to see it?" Doray asked but Misty just said "Come" and stepped toward the ship.

"Cool, you give your toys names." I was still a little nervous. "Hi ASTAR," I waved as I got near. "My father makes toys," I explained as we entered the ship. "Maybe he could help fix it for you."

"Yes, it is broken," said Comcom. "And I am afraid we have broken the crystal. It is what makes it go. So now we must grow another one."

Never had I imagined such an amazing toy. Great curved walls covered in a blanket of tiny lights. Then, almost as though it were a thought, a galactic map appeared in the air. A swirling cosmos of snow like a whirlpool glided through the room. Comcom stepped forward and asked, "Would you like to know where we are in this galactic snowball?"

"Oh. You mean this is home?" I asked. It was a little confusing. "It is one dimension of your many homes," he said. I thought he sounded kind of excited. I must have looked a little puzzled because Doray interrupted saying, "Don't get the lad confused with other dimensions right now. Let's keep it simple."

Lifting his finger, Doray sifted down into the cloud and found what he called our "solar system." It was just a tiny dot. Then he somehow made it bigger so I could see our sun and the other planets revolving around it. "The priests say the world is the center of everything," I commented.

"It is only their belief," commented Misty. "When they get wiser, they will travel, as we do, and then they will know more." Doray was making a motion with his finger and the circle of our earth around the sun began to show up as a golden thread.

Elfin world is near that star over there," he said as he again sifted down into the cloud and found a little pin dot. "ASTAR brings us through a portal in time so it is no distance at all."

"You can see through into it if you want to," Misty queried. "Wow. Amazing!" I was looking into a window in which I could see right into their world, which she called "Elfin." It had great dwellings and beautiful homes in wonderful forestland. Trees grew there, much larger than our own, and seemed to cover their entire planet.

It was an exciting and totally natural world. Then I noticed that the people were smaller than humans. "How come everyone is smaller than me?" I asked. "Our size has many advantages in our world," replied Misty. "But, in this world, life is organized a little differently. Let us show you."

At this point, each of the Elves took a place around the holoscope. Moving his fingers like a pianist playing a piano, they began to unfold a series of moving three-dimensional pictures that seemed to appear at the command of their fingers.

Delicate crystals appeared at various places spinning, as if in space, within the holoscope. Between the crystals formed different patterns that turned into life-like forms that looked every bit like they were living at that moment. The holoscope took on the form of a great Elfin eye. What must have been ancient art, so complex yet so simple, was mixed with wisdom and technology beyond anything humans had ever conceived. I was overawed. "I wish I knew all about everything." I said in my innocence.

"We are willing to share what we know, Nicholas, at least to the extent we are allowed," said Misty. "You humans live on a life planet. Look. See how life forms on your world," said Doray. Then, as though we were flying over the Earth, I watched as he showed me hundreds of different life forms, in all their colors and varieties. "Oh! What is that?" I asked. I was fascinated by any huge fish that swam near the top of the ocean.

"That is a school of whales. Magnificent, aren't they?" Comcom replied. "How is it that life has so many different kinds?" I was looking at all the plants, the bugs and animals. It seemed like there were so many different kinds! I never knew. I had never realized it before. "How come?" I wanted to know.

Misty held up her hand and the panorama stopped. "All intelligence arises from one source of life." The picture changed. Suddenly, all life forms fit as though on a great tree. "This is sometimes called the Tree of Life," she almost whispered. "Each life form organizes into its very own type but all are the same." I watched as the image seemed to focus on my hand. Then it went inside my hand, showing my skin, then below my skin. "Look," she said, "Watch how everything is made of information. Even your hand." The holoscope kept probing deeper and deeper into my hand. It seemed able to go into layers and layers of smallness until finally it showed spinning bits of sparklets. "See – information!" she declared. "See how it flows like a wave?"

"It's like a whirlpool!" I exclaimed. "My Dad showed me how water forms into whirlpools but I never knew my hand was made of little whirlpools!"

She continued as the other Elves kept their fingers busy on the holoscope. "Now watch," she encouraged me, "as intelligence breaks up the wave into harmonic spinning units. It is beautiful because every part has its own harmonic." I watched as the Elves showed me how small, cyclic waves of information formed into energy spinners and took form in space and time, as well as how these smallest forms shaped the particles that made up atoms, molecules and protein strings.

"See these strings?" Doray asked. I looked and there, forming in front of my eyes, was a twisted ladder with lots of rungs in it. "That will be called 'the double helix loop' in the future," Misty whispered. "It is your information control center that builds your body. In fact," Comcom said, "every animal and plant has one and everyone's is unique."

"Look at that!" I exclaimed as I looked at a beautiful jelly fish anchored on a magnificent coral reef and surrounded by myriads of fish. The scene changed and great flocks of birds, like waves of molecules all begin to circle, forming energy fields which turn in upon themselves and then, in turn, taking on various shapes without disconnecting from the information field.

"Now watch" said Misty. "All the harmonics come into what we call 'orchestration.' They all join into bigger and bigger harmonics. Each level is another expression of intelligence. Everything is alive. All matter is alive. This is why you can communicate with all matter. Your mind and all matter are part of the same harmonic. They all speak the same language if you know how to tune in," continued Misty.

"It is beyond my wildest dreams!" It was the most beautiful thing I had ever seen, so filled with color and so dynamic that I was mesmerized by its magnificence. "Life is *one* everywhere and 'every-when,' all one, interacting system," Misty said. "Even the life in our galactic system is one with life here. It is the same force and it is formed outside of time and space."

I could have watched the living screen forever. It was the most beautiful thing I had ever seen. I could go inside it. All I had to do was stick my head inside the mist. I could see anything I focused on and I could see how it was made, how it lived and thought and how it took its form. Finally, the Elves persuaded me to step away from the central control panel of the holoscan.

"Let us show you how your own body is made," Misty exclaimed. "It's very interesting!" My body came up on the screen. I could see my heart pumping and all the blood moving through my veins. They took me inside my eye. My eyelid had more little blood vessels than any other part of my body! It looked like a little blotch of red threads woven together into a little network. Then we went into my retina, my fovea and periphery. Everything was covered with little screens. Some were larger than others. "See how this little pin dot back in your eye picks up particle information while your whole inside of your eye picks up waves?" It was Doray again. "This little pin dot is what people will come to call your fovea. Look at these little screens covering your fovea."

I looked and, sure enough, there was a fine-screened filter over my fovea. "And look at these covering your periphery!" Misty piped in. "Well, I can see them but they look different – bigger," I noticed.

"Right you are!" replied Comcom. They were all gathered around looking in detail at my eye. "The fine-grained screens of your fovea let in particle information. The gross-grained screens let in waves." I just looked at Doray like he was speaking in Greek. "It's all holographic!" Doray almost shouted.

"Look." They showed me how my nervous system carries the information into my brain where it is connected into a holographic network. "Here are your memory units – 'holodynes' - self-organizing information systems. They are like little entities inside you. They pass on from generation to generation and they control much of human behavior," said Comcom.

"Look," he said. I watched as the pictures took on a different color. "Down into your cells go your nerves and right into your microtubules and then into your harmonics. See these little microtubules?" He was pointing with his finger to some small things that looked like long cobs of corn. "That is where intelligence stores its memory and connects with life energies," Comcom explained. Even though Comcom was speaking in big words, I seemed to sense what he was saying. My mind, I noticed, was working in pictures.

He went on. "Those are quantum fields of potential intelligence. They store all the wave and particle energy forms from your body. It is the same for most life forms. It is also the source of your power as a person." I could not understand his big words but I watched as the pictures flew in front of me.

From the eye of the computer screen emerged holographic images of all the parts of my body. I could see for the first time how life forms can be shown in diagrams. "My father draws like this on paper to make my toys." My body seemed to be made up of many different kinds of smaller life forms.

"Let's take a look at your brain," continued Comcom. They did what they called "a brain scan." As I looked on, the little party of Elves began talking all at once. "Look how alert!" cried Doray. "How much intelligence is manifesting," said Comcom. "Ohhh. He is so open!" exclaimed Solah. "And what a great interest he has in learning," Mefa continued. I was just getting embarrassed when Misty spoke up.

"Why," said Misty, "he's a Sender!" The Elves stopped suddenly. Their attention riveted on me. "What is a SENDER doing here?" she asked. "And at this time?" Comcom mused. "This must be a lot bigger than we thought. I wonder if parallel time dimensions are slicing into our field?" questioned Mefa.

"I sensed something very special about him the moment I saw him," remarked Misty. "Let's take a closer look at him and see if we can figure out what makes him tick." She gave a questioning look at me. I looked at her, deeply into her eyes. I did not know what to say, but I suddenly realized both the Dwarf and the Griff had said the same thing. I was a "Sender." Before I could ask her more about it, the computer screen switched.

They scanned my microtubules, as they called them, where all my memories are stored and where my field connects to the whole field. Suddenly, they came across the memory banks of the monastery.

They grew serious. Now this is strange for the Elves since they are mostly happy. But when they looked upon the torture chamber and saw the dwarf, the silence grew heavy. They continued to watch as I encountered the inquisitional trial, the sweatshop and finally the Griffs.

"He has touched the entropy force and is not prepared," said Misty. Then Comcom said, in a reflective voice, "This world is vulnerable to black hole invasion by the Delovians."

"Examine that crystal more closely," suggested Doray, pointing his finger toward the crystal that had spilled into my back pack. "It appears Delovian. It is associated with information monitoring and energy transformation," said Mefa. "Note how it responds to Nicholas." They watched as I talked to the Griffs. "Check to see who is monitoring it," said Comcom.

"It's Dwarg!" whispered Misty, and they all grew silent. "This means the Delovians are breaking the intergalactic prime directive." Comcom reached over and adjusted the holoscan.

"They are interfering with a life planet," he said, and everyone nodded in agreement. "Probably, were the ones who disrupted the tractor beam. That would make sense. But why would they dare to do it?"

After a moment, Mefa surmised "They would have to have a reason to impact the life flow. Tractor crystals can be contaminated if the life energy balance is disrupted during the fueling period."

"But that means they are breaking the Covenant and deliberately contaminating our crystal!" replied Doray. "It also might mean something even more sinister," remarked Solah. There was a long silence.

"What?" I asked. They shook their heads. "Tell me!" I said. "It's my mind you are reading. I have a right to know."

"He is a Sender. I guess it's OK." Comcom and Doray shook their heads in agreement but reluctantly. For a moment no one spoke. Then Misty stepped toward me. "The Delovians are advance troops for the black hole," she said.

"The black hole?" I questioned. "Yes." She saw the puzzled look on my face and she continued. "The black hole *eats* entire star systems. It can eat a whole galaxy - including all the stars in the sky."

"In one meal?" I asked. They laughed. I didn't know anything about black holes. I didn't know how big they were or what they were made of. I wanted to know. "No, not in one bite," Misty chuckled. "It takes thousands of years but, once the black hole tunes into a galaxy, if it has a strong enough death wish, it …" she hesitated. "It invites the black hole to come to it so it can die," replied Comcom.

"If the black hole is tuned in to this galaxy," concluded Mefa, "it can sense how strong the Grid of Agony is so it can tell how many people secretly wanted to die." I was beginning to get the picture. Agony would draw the black hole and the black hole would eat the world!

"The fact that Dwarg is here means they have sent one of their forward scouts to appraise the situation," continued Mefa. "However, Dwarg seems to be doing more than just observing," added Misty. "He seems to be involved in the torture and in the running of the Black Stone Monastery," said Doray. "Which means he is creating war!" concluded Comcom.

"Or, even worse" suggested Mefa, "the war is already going on!" Everyone was silent for a moment. Then Comcom spoke up. "He is creating a field into which the Black Hole will flow."

"Which means we get to find the solution that caused this problem," replied Misty. They were silent again, each lost in their own private thoughts. "I think it is right in front of us," said Misty. The Elves looked at me, and I drew away from the pictures on the holoscan. I wondered if I had done something wrong. "I didn't do it!" was my first response.

"It may well be," replied Comcom. "Just what do we really have here?" They turned back to the holoscan and began twisting their fingers through the field. I think they just kept probing my mind. "Why, he's still in resonate state!" Misty whispered. "Yes. But he is definitely a Sender," put in Mefa.

I was just about to ask what a Sender is when Mefa said, "It is amazing that humans would have emerged to the collective state of having Senders so soon in their development." Then Comcom pointed to a point in the holoscan. "Actually, our monitor shows Sender potential in every human but, in most generations, look at this – it appears that humans have not yet evolved to honor Senders or use them for their potential value."

"Perhaps that is something that could change," suggested Misty. "If they could learn to impact the Grid of Agony, they could reverse the death force."

"It would take Senders. Look at how this grid grows" pointed out Doray. "Humm," remarked Comcom. "Perhaps, under the Delovians, the Grid of Agony has become a tool. Within a few centuries...let's figure it out...there. Look at how the Grid of Agony grows."

Upon the holoscan, the world appeared with blotches of darkness. Like a cloud, small at first, a number of dots could be seen growing across the face of every land like a rising thunderstorm. "Look at the pollution!" Comcom said. "Look at how their cities begin to kill all other life. Look at how life slowly slips away. If conditions remain the same, all life on earth will end by the year ... it looks like about 2012 or 2020." Again, an ominous silence filled the little starship.

After awhile, Comcom continued: "Let us begin where we are and trust in life. Life has been around a long time." He turned to me. "Nicholas, look at this. See this dark cloud? See how fast the cloud is growing. It is what we call *the Grid of Agony*. As humans cause each other to suffer, their suffering affects the life force. So the more suffering, the more cloud. The more cloud, the more death. The more death, the closer comes the black hole. Do you understand?"

"I think so," I replied. "So the sadder people are and the meaner they are to each other, the sicker the world gets." I think I was catching on. "Good boy. Now look at this," he continued. "As we go back in history, we can trace how great the Grid of Agony has been in every generation. It has been growing. Now it is growing very fast and, if we project this into the future, watch how it continues to grow. By the year 2020, all life on the planet could end."

"Ai. You mean the world will die?" I was suddenly afraid - not just for myself, but for the children and people and plants and animals all over the world. "Yes. The world will die," he murmured. "What can we do?" I asked, almost too frightened to think about it. "Well, we have to look at what makes a difference to this grid. Let's see what we can find," replied Comcom. Everyone leaned forward into the holoscan.

"Look. There's a place where it went way down. What is causing that?" I asked. "Well, let's take a look," Comcom replied. "The screen shows a rapid decline in the Grid of Agony at several points in history. Let's take a look at that one."

"It appears, at that time, something happened that caused the grid to collapse," observed Mefa. "It was another Sender," Misty replied almost in a whisper. "What's a Sender?" I finally got to ask. "Well, let's take a look!" said Comcom.

"If you place your head in here, ASTAR will take you wherever you think about," explained Misty. I hesitated. She sensed my hesitation, "ASTAR, with what you already know about Nicholas, can you let him be captain for this next journey?"

"I would be honored," a voice replied. It sounded just like my father and I immediately knew all would be well. Misty sat me down in her chair. "Just clear your mind of all thoughts and feelings and lean forward so your head enters the holographic screen. It's easy and pretty much automatic."

I sat down and, taking a deep breath, leaned forward. The holoscreen was warm and molded itself around my face and head. Small little needles of energy, which did not hurt at all, pushed themselves onto the surface of my skin. "Now, think, and the computer will respond," ordered Comcom.

I thought of all the children in the sweatshop laundry of the Black Stone Monastery. Immediately, I could see into the sweatshop. "Whoa," said Doray. "Not yet. It will take some experience to get them out of there."

"But they want to be free," I pleaded. "We know," he replied. "Let's do first things first. OK?" He looked over at Misty. "Now Senders," Misty explained "can travel through time. They are able to travel in parallel times. And maybe you could learn to do it." She smiled as she looked over at me. "Ai, what is it?" I asked. "It's like popping in and out of a room, only you pop in and out of time," Misty remarked.

"Ai, that would be interesting. When do I get to do it?" I was getting excited. "We'll see. Let's see if we can find what caused the grid to get so small here..." She moved the screen over a map, "It seems to be coming from here...." She moved the monitor over... "A small town in.... There we have it. It's a little place called Bethlehem, 1,482 years ago."

"Why it's coming from a little human baby," said Misty. A scene arose on the screen in which a baby is being birthed in a manger. It is a very tender scene and very real, but it is shadowed by a dark cloud. "The Grid of Agony!" Comcom gasped. It began to fade in and out, like a storm coming over a mountain.

"The grid makes it difficult. We would have to be there to really get the information we need," he said. What about it ASTAR?"

"Can we really go visit them?" I wanted to go. It was the first time I had ever seen a baby born and I knew he must be very special. Everything in my being wanted to be there. "We are locked into your space-time but we can travel within it," Misty replied.

"Actually," says Comcom, "it might be necessary in order to get a pure fix on the frequency of information coming from that Sender. He is beautiful, and we don't want the grid to interfere. Mefa, check and see if we can get the coordinates to transport to that time and place. And Misty," Comcom paused, seeming to listen within himself, and then, giving a little nod of his head he said, "perhaps we should check on our friend in our parallel time."

Paaaiiinnn! The giant Benton continues to turn the rack wheel. "Soon we will rule the entire world. First, we must get rid of all those who do not think right - like you." I wanted to scream from the agony and pain but my mind takes me back - back to my father. "Oh, sweet Jesus" he says, "Please come unto me."

My father is finishing the buckle. A flash of memory occurs in my father's mind as he looks at the intricately designed reindeer and sleigh with a little person dressed in a parka. "I'm a Santa, I'm a Santa. Look, Father."

"So many years ago," I said to myself as I am being stretched on the rack. "My birthday – 15 years ago. It seems like only yesterday." As my father finished fashioning the belt buckle on which he engraved the miniature picture of Santa and a sleigh with eight tiny reindeer, I can still see its fine-crafted artistry.

A silver buckle that captured the magic moment between father and son when they flew down the mountain together in the fantasy of flying, being pulled by magic reindeer. "Look, Father!! I'm a Santa!! I'm a Santa!!!"

The belt buckle passed in front of my memory and with it came the memory of Malevolent, within the inquisition chambers. I can hear the all-male choir practicing its beautiful music in the monastery's choral chambers. Malevolent and 12 priests dressed in black are gathered in the courtroom. A map of the world as it is known is spread in gothic print across a wall. Dwarg, the dwarf, is explaining the power centers that have been established in every part of the world and is telling them to prepare for the new world order and the discovery of a new land that is about to take place.

A report is being given to the group of priests in another section of the chamber. All are rigid, hard and serious. The report is on a satanic happening that must be purged.

"There are ordinary people undermining the powers of God. Here is how you can recognize them." He shows a list: no payment of tithes to the monastery, no attendance at daily Mass, no weekly confessions, no baptism of children, attempting to make earth metals celestial, which was never meant to be, so that they float in the air. This undermines the word of God since all solid objects must flow down and any attempt to stop this downward flow is of the Devil because it steals the power of God. Here are samples of satanic devices." He shows them a cupboard filled with kites and other floating objects.

The priest who spied upon the father's workshop hurries into the room. "Malevolent, your holiness, an audience?" And then Malevolent's sharp reply: "What is it, Father?"

"In the smithy shop in the valley of Holy Grace, I saw with my own eyes such floating objects. And I saw the Satanic symbols of which the teacher talks. They were lying around the Devil's workshop. I personally witnessed an arrow that floated."

As he talks, Malevolent pauses to signal Dwarf. He listens and says, "Good. Now the flames will spread. We must recover the transceiver crystal. At least we know where it is and by tonight we will be on our way."

"Do not delay," says the Dwarf. "Every moment that transceiver is in the hands of the Sender, we are cut off and vulnerable. You must act quickly."

"It will be done, my Lord," whispers Malevolent. He raises his arms. All priests stop talking and turn in his direction. "We will go down" he says, "and we will deal with the Satan worshipers now. Gather together your truth-teller tools and prepare to defend the kingdom of God. Let us purge the world of the evil doers - those who are trying to capture the power of God, to be used for evil purposes."

Pulling Benton the Giant aside, he whispers, "Together we will lead a group of the holiest of men and get these satanic instruments and burn them and then hold an inquisition. We must destroy those who oppose God."

They gather their torture-to-truth tools - the thumbscrews, the head vices and the nail pressers. The dwarf smiles as they leave the monastery and begin the short journey to our home.

In the cave, I was invited to step outside the starship for some lessons. I was being taught by Doray to levitate objects by the use of a star crystal strapped to the inside of my wrist. I was bouncing little rocks into the air. They were jumping everywhere. All went well, I thought, until one bounced off the starship. Then another showered over Comcom as he stepped from the ship. He turned and put his hands on his hips. Looking at Misty, he said, "I realize he is learning how to use it, perhaps outside the cave?" Misty nodded and directed me outside. As we left the cave, I noticed it was getting late.

"I must be home before dark or father will worry." I wasn't sure of the way. "I will walk back with you," Misty reassured me. "Elves do not have to sleep. I have to get used to the idea that humans need sleep."

"Oh" was all I could say. I didn't know much about Elves. I didn't know they didn't sleep. "How old are you?" I asked. "In earth years? Well... that's hard to say. Elves don't get old unless they are locked in time."

"Are you locked in time now?" I found everything about Elves as wonderful. "Yes, I guess we are. But don't you worry," she reassured me, "there never was a problem that was not caused by its solution." I looked at her a little confused. "But maybe the grid will get you?" I said with a questioning tone. "I think being in your time is where we are supposed to be right now, so don't worry, OK?" She looked up at me and gave me such a smile that I knew everything would be all right.

We continued on the path back to my home and I was bouncing everything I could think of into the air. Little twigs leapt up before me. A squirrel, jumping from one branch to another was suddenly lifted into the air. As it catapults off the branch in surprise, it found itself lifted gently back as I swooped it up onto the branch again. "Ho, Ho, Ho! What fun!" I could not have imagined a better toy.

As we rounded the bend, coming into sight of my valley, I paused. Misty stood facing me, her great almond eyes penetrating into me. She took me by both hands. Looking deeply into her eyes, I knew she knew. I really did not want to leave my new friends. I sighed and began to undo the wrist levitator. But Misty stopped me.

"Why don't you keep it for awhile — until you can come back and visit us again?" she asked. "Oh could I really? Oh really? It's the best birthday gift I ever got. Oh this is so great! Ho! Ho! Ho!" I guess I must have jumped around a bit much but finally I leaned down and twirled her around giving her a big kiss on the cheek.

She gently held me and the loving energy that poured from her was like a light in the night. With twinkling eyes she said, "Perhaps tomorrow?"

I nodded and waved, "Tomorrow."

"He took the levitator. OK. How are the toys coming? We'll need them right away. They will need to be exact duplicates. And can we get back to Bethlehem?" Comcom is intense.

Doray is adamant. "We're working on it chief. Working from real time is tricky though but we should be able to do it with help."

"With help? From whom?" asks Comcom.

"From the two Senders we have found among the humans. The computer scene shows Nicholas descending down through the forest toward his home and the baby Jesus in his mother's arms," reports Doray.

As I descended into my valley and was approaching the stream, the priests of the inquisition were stealthily positioning themselves in the shadows of the trees as close to my father's smithy shop as they could get without being detected. Hidden in the shadows, they waited.

Unaware of their presence, I called to my father. "Father? Father? Are you ready?" I called. My father stepped out of the shop and waved me forward. "Ho, Ho, Ho!" he chuckled. "All is ready." His laughter lightened my heart and lifted my spirits as he stepped into the shop and brought out the puffer into which he then fitted the arrow. With the priests watching — I must have passed within a few feet of them, but so intent was I upon my father, that I did not notice them — I riveted my eyes to my father's every move.

Just as I ran onto the open meadow, he let the arrow fly. He had tied the silver buckle to the arrow and now, as it flew up, up into the air, it lifted all eyes to its course. As it reached its pinnacle against the blue, it puffed into a silver parachute. A gasp uttered from every priest. The priests drew their crosses, holding them between themselves and the floating evil arrow.

The Starship

Chapter Six

The Death of a Sender

I swept into the meadow, squealing with delight and ready to catch the slowly descending arrow. The priests had seen enough. As one man, they rose from the shadows and stepped forth as inquisitors. They were still unnoticed as I positioned myself under the descending arrow and dashed in at the last moment to catch it. Clutching the arrow to my breast, I looked down and saw the buckle tied to the arrow. "Oh father," I exclaimed, looking up at him. "It is wonderful."

I was still examining the wonder of the belt buckle when Malevolent came up behind me, grabbed me by the back of the neck and yanked the arrow and buckle from my hands. "Ouch. That hurt!" I retorted squirming around to see who was so rude.

The inquisitors stormed the barn and took my father prisoner. In the struggle, he shouted, "Run! Nicholas run!" I was only able to squirm free for a moment and Malevolent caught me firmly by the hair.

He dragged me back to the inquisitors where a scene of unparalleled horror occurred — one that I have never been able to forget. I was forced to watch as they put the thumb screws and the head vice on my father torturing him. I marveled at his strength and courage. His eyes never left mine. "Do not forget: I love you" they seemed to say. "Do not forget: I love you."

Malevolent searched the barn and found the dark crystal. He put it inside his robe and returned to the torture scene with a look of total triumph. "A Sender, huh? We shall see, we shall see."

I could not forget the look my father held on me. Through the pain his eyes forever told me of his love. He and I both knew he was a dead man. He was signaling me to get away if I could. It was growing dark. They accused my father of satanic worship and delving into the mysteries of God and trying to steal the power of God. They asked if these instruments belonged to him. He said, "Yes. I made them. They are toys."

"It is enough," said Malevolent. He declared my father a Satan worshiper and condemned him to death. I screamed my objections and told them they were all the Satan worshipers. They placed a gag upon my mouth and made me watch as the priests gathered all my toys and my father's tools into a pile next to the shop. They tied him to a beam on the outside of the shop and gathered hay and wood.

Malevolent himself struck the flint that started the fire. I wanted to look away, but Malevolent forced my face to watch and even though I closed my eyes, I could still see the fire and hear the final screams as my whole life was burned away.

I went cold and numb.

Paaaiiinnn again. I am back on the rack in the torture chamber. I scream my rage and pain. "That's it. Give yourself over to the agony. You the Sender! You can send agony. Ha, Ha, Ha. You can send agony. Death to the Elves and death to all Senders. Ha, Ha, Ha! Death to life. Ha, Ha, Ha!" Comes the Black Hole. Comes the Black Hole!" screams the Dwarf.

Then, from deep within: "Remember. Every problem is a solution waiting to be born." I can see the eyes of Misty and hear her voice but still the pain persists. "Nooooo!" I scream as the pain fries at my nerve endings.

"Embrace the pain." It is a man's voice. "Take my love upon you." A bright light floods my mind. An overwhelming love, so peaceful I am awestruck. My pain is instantly overshadowed. The rack becomes as nothing. I find myself walking with my father in a place of peace and light. So relieved am I that I seem to flow into the love of my father.

"I love you Father." The words are as nothing to what I am experiencing. "I love you my son." His voice is so reassuring that I forget all about my pain. Then beside us, walks another being. "Allow your mind to be at peace," he reassures me. "Your powers are amplified when you are in harmony. They are diminished when you are in agony or anger."

I know he is right. I look at my father. "But, Father, they killed you. They took everything from me. I was only a boy. They deserve to die. Their order deserves to die. It created such evil."

Suddenly my hate brings me completely into the Grid of Agony. I can see myself using the wrist levitator to throw them all screaming into the flames. Yet, it is as though I am watching myself. It isn't really me.

"Hate is a finite game in which no one can ever win and all will surely lose." It is my father's voice and yet it is also the voice of others. "I know father. It is all right. I live beyond the game and beyond the pain."

"Love is the answer," he replies. "Love is the answer. His love." He pointed over to a group of people gathering around Jesus. He waves and they all look and wave joyfully toward me. One very beautiful woman rises and starts toward me and I think I recognize her but she is stopped by a look from Jesus. I go to join her but I am suddenly back on the rack. Then through the cloud of black pain in which I am almost consumed comes a voice:

"Remember who you are and the power of love. Remember his love and the love you are." Those words keep bringing me back, remembering what happened.

At the height of the roaring flames, Malevolent suddenly realized he was still holding the puffer. He throws it with the belt buckle tied to it, into the flames.

As the puffer hit the heat wave, it puffed open and floated for a moment in the air above the fire. The priests were alarmed and stepped back, drawing their crosses. Malevolent let go of me and did the same. For one moment I was free.

In that moment, as the flames began to dissolve the arrow and, at the last second, just as the flames surrounded the buckle, I lifted my wrist and directed the levitator crystal toward the buckle. It caught the buckle that flipped upward, out of the flames and through the night air. It landed beyond the fire in the dust unseen by the priests.

I was numb, a hardness having come over me at such a tender age. I could still hear Malevolent's words as I watched my father die, "When you grow up, you become a Priest. If you want to meddle with the powers of God, you must do it in God's way, through the Church, and not in Satan's way through these devices."

The priests formed a circle around the fire to do a cleansing chant and a purification prayer. I saw my chance and slipped back away from them into the forest, under cover of the dark. No sooner had I stepped into the shadows than one of the priests shouted, "The boy! Where is the boy?!"

"That whelp of Satan has escaped. Find him!" shouted Malevolent. They took torches and began searching into the forest. As silently as I could, I crawled deep under the ferns. Whenever a priest came close to me, I would take my levitator and point it at things that were away from me. I would move them and the small noises would distract the priest away from my place. Gradually I slipped further into the darkness of the forest.

It became too dangerous with torches in the woods and they had to put out several small fires when I lifted up bunches of leaves into the path of their flames. It kept them away. Then suddenly one of the priests yelled, "Fire! The forest is on fire!" I could not see it, well-hidden as I was, but the light of a growing forest fire soon rose above the light from the burning of my home.

"Back to the monastery! Run! We must get out of the forest or we will be burned alive!" Malevolent was shouting. "We go!" shouted Benton, and they went like shadows before the light disappearing into the darkness over the meadow. The last to go were Malevolent and Benton. Finally, knowing they couldn't find me, Benton said, "We'll come back and get him in the morning. The sweatshops will be a fit place for him." They left and I was completely alone.

I waited for what seemed a long time to make sure they were really gone and then, as the flames of the rapidly growing fire began to surround me, I walked slowly out of the forest and into the meadow. I could find no evidence left of the life I had lived with my father or any of my toys. All that remained was a burning ball of fire. Then, from the light of the flames I caught the reflection of something in the dust beyond the outer rim of the ashes. I went over and reached down. There in the dirt was the last remaining memory of my father, the belt buckle with the sleigh, the eight tiny reindeer and the word "SANTA" at the top.

I picked it up and turned it slowly in my hands. It was such a beautiful work of art. I remembered riding down the hill, my hands lifted above me, "I'm a Santa! I'm a Santa!"

Suddenly a priest rushed at me. "I've got you, whelp." But I raised the levitator and he was suddenly lifted beyond me and went crashing over my head into a smoldering tree.

Something inside of me began to break. I grasped the buckle to my heart and, from the light of the now raging fire in the trees surrounding the meadow, I looked once more upon the home I once had and down to the word "Santa," and the eight little reindeer with the sleigh and a great sob began from deep inside me. As the forest fire began to fill our little valley, I began to run, sobbing uncontrollably. I can remember crying and running, running, running. I cared not about the fire or my safety. I cared not about the world or its monasteries or of other worlds or of Elves or anything else. I cared for naught for life. I just ran and ran and ran until I was running beside myself.

It was as though I could see myself running, purging my mind and body and soul, draining the innocence of my childhood, the very metal of my being melting and forging a steel-hard band around my heart. I cast a solid iron cloak around me so that nothing would ever hurt this much again.

I ran through the forests, the once friendly ferns and branches of a once gentle forest, catching at me, slapping me, scratching and stinging me at every step. I ran and ran, the fire still raging all around me. I was oblivious to everything, drowning in my own sorrow, my soul searching some sort of cleansing only a Sender could seek and experiencing the pain of immersion into the deepest places within the Grid of Agony. Forging from the flaming forest of my mind was that refining fire that transforms mere mortals into Senders.

I ran blindly through the woods with no thought of time. The agony of my losses was so overwhelming that I could not extinguish its flames or escape its suffocation. Forest ferns and branches beat me down; exhaustion and smoke smothered me; darkness enveloped me; and flames surrounded me, lapping up the air. On and on I ran and ran, trying to escape from the beast of rage and the anguish of agony.

I ran until I could run no more. I had no knowledge that I had outrun the fire, no knowledge that I was near the cave. I collapsed into unconsciousness and drowned in my sorrow, numbing me from the grinding Grid of Agony in which I was consumed and leaving me without awareness of the galactic war into which I had been thrust at such a young and tender age.

"We will let you rest awhile," says Benton as he releases me from the tension of my chains upon the rack. "After all, we can't have you passing out before you have properly experienced all the pain. Ha! Ha! Ha!" The giant clamps my wrists into the wall chains, yanks the chains and lifts me harshly against the wall. I hung from chains through two rings on the wall. "No escaping now. Ha! Ha!" he roared as he left the room. I am left alone, barely alive.

Scene after scene passes through my mind. As Kris Kringle, I remember visiting city after city, sweatshop after sweatshop, in country after country. I remember making toys for children and being thrown out of town after town for causing "pernicious thoughts of play" among the young.

I see that priests operate in every village and town across the land. Inquisitors, witch burners and missionaries sent by the Black Monastery begin to take power everywhere. The map of conquests continually grows in the Black Stone Monastery. Its markers stretch into China and Japan. Absolute control by the Church completely covers Europe, Russia, Persia and most of Africa. The Middle East and India are swept before it. Missionaries answer the call like swarms of black locusts they descend upon every village, every town and every city.

Missionaries are everywhere. I can hear their voices: "We shall soon have absolute power. Now is the day of the power of the priest. Now is the day when none can stand against us. We will purge the world and set the standard of the Lord for all to see," Malevolent shouts to a great crowd of new recruits.

"Yes," growls Dwarg. "The standard of the Lord." Turning to the crowd of new recruits, he shouts: "Purge the world. Cleanse the field. Reap the harvest."

Long lines of new priests raise their arms and shout: "Reap the harvest." They are dressed in white. Washed in the water from the river of the monastery, they are made to kneel and pledge everything to the kingdom of God or they will have their throats slit. They are burned with the brand of the cross and then a gray robe is placed upon them, the Initiates.

Long lines of women file through a separate chamber. "You are now wedded to the Christ. Repeat after me: 'I will never have sexual relationships with any of the sons of Adam. I will never think carnal thoughts. Rather than do so, I would suffer my life to be taken." Each woman makes a cutting motion with her hand across her throat. "I will devote my life to God and to His Church. I will never own any earthly thing. I will never covet any other person's earthly goods. I will never lie except in the defense of the kingdom of God and I will never keep any truth from the father's confession. I will never disobey a priest. Rather than do so, I would suffer my life to be taken. God is good, God is good, God is good."

Benton, who is returning me to the rack, brings my reverie back to an awareness of my situation in the chamber. "Wouldn't want you to get too comfortable. Ha, Ha," he laughs. The pain begins again. My mind goes back, back, back.

Comcom buried his face in the monitor of the computer. "ASTAR, let's take another look at the grid of human experience." His focus was complete. "Any particular aspect sir?" the computer responded. "Yes," replied Comcom. "I want to monitor the *collective sender*." Since there was still no response from ASTAR, Comcom continued; "It's collective consciousness. Let's check human growth as a culture and explore how it has evolved over history."

ASTAR still seemed a little mystified so Misty suggested: "Check our own location in time and see if anything is affecting the field." In a few moments Comcom pulled his head out of the monitor.

"Whew. There is a major virus here. The Grid of Agony is growing at an exponential rate. I am picking up a major addition to the grid not too far from the cave and there's a forest fire all around it. It's reading codes like that of Nicholas."

"Can you locate the exact source point?" asked Mefa. "Yes. It's right about there." He pinpointed the location and Misty said, "I think I will go and see what that is." She whisked herself out of the starship and walked quickly out of the cave and into the forest. Comcom put his head back into the holoscan.

Deep in the forest Misty found Nicholas unconscious. She quickly discovered that he was physically in shock but had no serious injuries. Using her levitator still attached to his wrist, she levitated him back to the starship and safely away from the fire. The Elves gathered around as she placed him on the scanning deck. "Let's take a look at what could have caused this," Comcom said. "Scanning," replied ASTAR.

Within the holoscan they watched as the events of night unfurled before them. The scenes that traumatized Nicholas' life were projected in detail before the horrified Elves from their fresh memory banks within his body where they had now been stored forever. "It is unbelievable that a life planet would be so primitive that adults would do this to a developing Sender," Misty said. "What is the source of this hate?" asked Mefa. "It is connected to the Grid of Agony, that's for sure," said Comcom.

"Look at this, Sir," reported Tedo. "Within the grid there appears to be a primary source of the agony." "Yes," said Solah. "It is the black crystal and..." he paused a moment, "it seems to be connected to another dimension."

"Can we trace it?" asked Comcom. "I have already done it. I traced a random access right to... this particular part of this galactic system." He pointed to a black void in the ocean of stars.

"Any peculiar characteristics about this part of the galactic system?" asked Comcom. "I am afraid so." There was a long pause before Tedo could bring himself to say anything. Finally: "It provides a door to a parallel antimatter dimension. It's the entry to a black hole."

"They are connecting life matter with anti-matter!" exclaimed Comcom. "Oh, NOOOooo. Then they WILL be able to end life on earth!" cried Misty. "Anti-matter could do it. The way they've hooked this up, its purpose is to transform life energy on the planet into a parallel world. They could eventually suck the entire galaxy into an anti-matter black hole." Comcom voiced the concern of all. "Life on earth won't have a chance. Our life crystal, Elfin world and everything would go," he said.

"The death of the galaxy and the birth of a black hole," cried Misty. "How can we possibly find a solution while locked into linear time? It is so...so...human!"

"But it is interesting to find out how they seed the black hole and eat a world and then a galaxy," commented Mefa. "Perhaps, we can scan the agony grids for all the children on the planet and project what will happen if the Grid of Agony continues to grow?" His suggestion riveted them.

The Elves bent over into the holoscan. There, within the holoscan, they witnessed the plight of the children. Most appeared in terrible agony. In every city, they were deprived, abused and abandoned and they were put into slave labor. "Look!" observed Doray: "When their parents object they are brought before the inquisition and punished or worse, tortured and burnt at the stake. Their children are put in the sweatshops and forced to work. This is worse than anything we could have imagined."

"We'd better get serious," replied Comcom. "Better still, we'd better enter the game. We can play this game. Let's begin by projecting that Grid of Agony into the future."

But Doray objected. "Look," he said, "Nothing we have done so far has even begun to affect the grid. If these agony points continue in the grid of humanity, all life on the planet will end sooner than we projected."

Comcom asked, "What now? What are our options?" Doray suggested: "Well, the grid fluctuates, so there is something which keeps it from growing, something that stops it. If we could seed the agony points at the appropriate entry time in life, then the seeding process would put whatever was needed into the grid."

"Everything can be reduced to mathematics," piped in Solah. "Everything can be reduced to music," Mefa reminded him. Suddenly they all seemed to relax and quit spontaneously. The four Elves, Doray, Mefa, Solah and Tedo began to sing.

"We'll start at the very beginning,
"It's a very good place to start."

As the four Elves sang, the rising crescendo of their harmony drew out of the holoscan the beginning of all forms of life. From the first geometrics, Comcom outlined the spinning torus, the geometric design from which all things emerge. Then, with his finger, he drew out the golden mean and placed it upon the torus. From the interaction of the two, the creation of all mathematical geometric shapes sweeping forward into variations of colors and creating the harmonics of every atom, molecule and even the DNA that then emerged into all information systems and life forms. It was a work of art!

This harmonic of information vibrated joyfully, creating standing waves at each point, which then appeared as matter. The whole field erupted with "white holes" in the "quantum foam."

"Human intelligence affects the field according to focus," mused Comcom. "And the resonating wave that gives form to the images of reality and physical matter," added Misty. "Hate has one frequency and love another. The love frequency can absorb the hate frequency."

"Well since the love frequency can absorb the hate frequency, our first job," declared Doray, "is to find an entry point at which we can impact the Grid of Agony with a love frequency."

Then Misty got an idea, "I suggest we start with our little Sender, Nicholas."

"We'll never scan everything. It would take forever. We have to give ASTAR some reference point," Mefa observed. "This will take forever."

"His heart is so closed against the pain," Mefa remarked as he ran the holoscan over Nicholas. "There is no easy way through." Just then Misty noticed that Nicholas' fist was closed around something. She pried open his little unconscious fingers and found the belt buckle. Placing it in the center of the machine, she said, "Let's see what vibratory memories have been forged into this matter."

Projected into the time frame of the disc was a three-dimensional image of the mountain scene between Nicholas and his father. "I'm a Santa! I'm a Santa!" "He is grasping the belt buckle as a reminder," Misty observed. "Through it he can save his memory of the love he and his father have for each other. It is his anchor so he doesn't lose his sanity entirely."

She continued to explore his patterns. "He is so sensitive to collective dynamics. He knows the inquisitors killed his mother but he wasn't personally involved. She just disappeared and he was too young to know what happened. But now his father has also been killed and he realizes how bad it must have been for his mother."

"And he was not able to help," piped in Mefa. "Not his mother, nor the man in the monastery or his father. Now his mind is trying to grasp how the pain and evil of society needs to be dealt with. He is a Sender but he cannot figure it out yet."

"He knows nothing of the patterns by which the human mind grows," commented Solah. "It is orders within orders. He will need to learn about holodynes and how they mature. That's a great place to start."

"He already knows about love but, with this kind of trauma, it will take a miracle to pull him through," Doray said, in a tone that indicated he was just thinking out loud. "Look at this," Mefa reflected. "These immature holodynes pass on from generation after generation. They are the basis of how collective thought takes place and how immature holodynes create the Grid of Agony in the Field of Love. They have no self-disciplining process. The immature ones keep on passing on. They don't correct themselves on this planet unless someone actually chooses to love in spite of all the pain."

"Well, we know this," said Misty. "Every point of agony is an uncompleted act of love."

"I never could figure that out," Mefa bantered, egging Misty on. She looked up and caught the gleam in his eyes. "You know very well the natural harmony of growth gets broken and the act becomes malignant. It causes pain, sorrow, loss or devaluation. Humans give up their power to their immature patterns. But, if we could get into the intention of their crowns of light, we could harvest the seed of power in each case."

Chapter Seven

The Delovian Galactic Council

On the other side of the approaching Black Hole, the ruling council of the Delovian Empire was in session. Dwarg's body appears partially on a holoscan screen. "I dare not enter, my lords, because I am contaminated to appear as matter. While it is necessary in order for me to remain in this galaxy of matter, it is not possible for me to come completely into your presence without losing my contact here."

"Yes, yes Dwarg. We already know this. Report. How is the Grid of Agony on the Elfin fueling station, planet Earth?" The being who spoke appeared as a shadow being, partly transparent and shaped as a dwarf. His features were gothic and his eyes piercingly dark. He wore, upon his middle finger of his right hand, a ring that extended across his three-fingered hand and up his wrist onto his arm. He was obviously the head of the ruling Council of the Delovian Empire.

"It goes well, my lords. The grid's growth rate is sufficient that by the time the Elfin Galactic council discovers the crack in the cosmic egg, our armada should be well positioned to consume the galaxy within the Black Hole."

"Don't patronize us with such bland optimism. Just report the facts," the ruler demanded. "When is closure?"

"Closure has already taken place. The Grid of Agony is now self-perpetuating." Dwarg raised his head, proud of his accomplishments.

"Excellent. You have been enjoying your work, I take it. What about the source crystal?" The ruler raised his eyebrows. "Did you recover it?"

"Oh, I had almost forgotten about that, it seemed like such an insignificant event." Dwarg shuttered at his near failure.

"Have you lost your sense of reality?" the ruler shouted. "The loss of a seed would give the Elfin galaxy access to our source codes. If it gets into the hands of a knowledgeable Sender, we don't know what that would mean. If you cannot maintain a proper respect for your responsibilities, perhaps we should send Delpha in your place?"

Dwarg was stung by the insult. Humbled, he replied, "It will not be necessary, my lord. I have the crystal secured within the Black Stone Monastery. Somehow a small boy, a Sender, who is still in resonance, gained access to the monastery and was able to get the crystal and escape. But we traced him to his hideaway and have recovered the crystal so the source is secured."

"Then you have destroyed the Sender?" the ruler asked.

"No, my lord. He escaped into the forest, but I believe we have put into play something more powerful than his immediate destruction." Dwarg was confident he could succeed.

"What could possibly be more powerful than the destruction of a Sender?" the ruler asked. The entire council was growing agitated.

"We have caused him to enter into the Grid of Agony," replied Dwarg. When he got no immediate response, he continued, "where his powers become a part of the forces of entropy."

There was considerable murmuring amongst the council members. Then the ruler raised his voice: "Can you assure us this is so?"

"He is but a human child of six years who loved his father. We had his father tortured and burned to death. He was forced to watch. It was another human, the holy priest Malevolent, who did it in the name of the boy's God."

"You are getting quite a flair for style, Dwarg. Monitor this Sender and keep us informed. Now, as to the schedule. What is the projected date of destruction?" The ruler was adamant.

"It will self-destruct by the earth year 2100." Dwarg wanted to give himself plenty of time. This project depended upon human participation and he wanted it to be fail-free.

"It is not good enough. Move the date up to 2012," the ruler replied. It was as though he could read Dwarg's thoughts. Knowing it was useless to resist, Dwarg agreed. "It shall be done, my Lords."

"De-lov-i-an!" The ruler raised his arm.

"De-lov-i-an my lords!" replied Dwarg, as he disappeared back into earth spacetime. As the faded image of Dwarg disappeared from the council chambers, a powerful female dwarf arose. Like all Delovians, she, too, was a shadow being. Her countenance was so dark, it seemed as though she were capable of absorbing anything or anyone who opposed her way of thinking. She stood now, facing the council. With a powerful voice, she raged, "My lords, Dwarg is an incompetent! It is a mistake to leave one such as this in charge of such an important and profitable mission. We need assurance that his stumbling attempt to grow the grid will not fail."

"What makes you feel he is so incompetent?" asked one of the council members. "Because he does not know he is being monitored by the Elves!" she roared. The entire council flew into panic. "The Elves are monitoring Dwarg?" the ruler shouted. "How do you know this?"

"Because my armada is stationed on the outer rim of the black hole," she replied. "What! You dare to approach the domain of matter without this Council's explicit orders?" the Ruler shouted. But she replied with calm reassurance. "You will remember that we are under orders to proceed with regard to the Elfin galaxy. We proceeded to the limit of our authority and no further."

"You launched a probe! We gave no permission for the penetration until we are ready. You are walking on very dangerous edge, Delpha!" the Ruler raged. But, again, Delpha replied with calmness.

"We are able to monitor limited, matter-time continuums as routine surveillance. We sent a probe, completely undetected, to find out what the Elves were doing in that part of the galaxy. It was a standard precaution since one of our seeds was there. We were very lucky. As a routine measure, we dropped in on their life crystal when we knew they had scheduled a fueling. We found ASTAR and Comcom's team there."

She waited, but the council remained silent. "Dwarg had lost the seed to the Sender. We decided to look further and we wanted to monitor the Sender."

"Well, what has that to do with Elves?" the ruler asked. She continued: "The Elves have the Sender. And they are monitoring everything Dwarg is doing."

"Then the mission is lost. I've a good mind to just leave him there!" the ruler declared.

"It is not lost." All eyes turned to her. "My armada discovered the Elves fueling ASTAR, their most advanced starship. We caught them completely by surprise by using a shadowed ball of entropy. We collapsed them into earth time and destroyed their life crystal."

A gasp went up from the entire council. "Well done! Well done indeed! Have they discovered your presence yet?"

"No, my lords," she replied. "They are locked into time and cannot monitor the parallel dimensions from which we are randomly surveying their activities. We have an armada in place that can overpower anything they could possibly assemble even if they knew we were coming."

"Take no chances, Delpha!" the ruler warned. "This galaxy is one of the richest in potential we have within reach of our parallel dimensions, and we have been planning this for centuries. Let nothing escape your control."

"It will be done my lords and, I have a special surprise for the Elves."

"Which is...?" the ruler asked. "Sorry, my lords. I am sure you understand. We do not know how the Elves escaped our last forage into space," she said. "I will reveal it when the time comes. Until then, De-lov-i-an."

"Go with darkness, Delpha. De-lov-i-an!" The council rose as one and saluted her. "De-lov-i-an!"

She left the huge council chamber and was immediately whisked away in a flying whirlwind of darkness. She flew through a maze of buildings of living stone and dark glass formed to shape their master's needs. Rising into the air in great columns, the buildings served as conduits that facilitate rapid transportation channels, both rising into the air and passing into the ground.

Delpha's dark vehicle of mist rose above the compound of her city and darted across the great crystal plains of Delovia. Below, the city appeared no more than a miniature anthill compared to the huge mountains of crystal that surrounded her kingdom. Within the world of the Delovians, her small transporter of dark mist disappeared into a small black hole.

At the controls of her central command, she directed her holoscan to contact Dwarg. "Hello, my darling. You did so well before the council today. They are nervous about this absorption of the Elfin galaxy."

"Never fear, my lovely one," he said. "We shall soon be together again and I can torture you mercilessly." He grinned a twisted smile and reached up with both his hands as though he were grabbing her.

"Oh I shall love that," she purred. "You torture me with your absence now. Have we neutralized the Sender?"

"Which one?" he countered.

"Both would be best," she purred. "We have attacked the sight of his birth and had all the children killed. Even at that, we could not be sure he was killed. So we wrapped the power of his love within the cloth of blackness and are spreading the Grid of Agony in his name. That's pretty good, don't you think?"

"It is brilliant my love," he replied. "Even if the intergalactic council was to monitor the activities, there is no evidence that humans themselves were not to blame."

"Then," she asked, "What of Nicholas?"

"We have, as you know, pushed him into the grid by the death of his father and mother," said Dwarg. "We shall see how he survives. We almost had him in the snow slide but he escaped. Now the Elves have him but, thanks to you, their ship is locked in time and they are impotent."

"Are you aware, my darling, that Doray's team is there along with Comcom and Misty?" Delpha raised an eyebrow as she asked the question. Dwarg replied, "They are the Elves who were refueling? Worst of luck. They are worthy adversaries indeed. I think this time we have them trapped in this space-time continuum. Ha. I'll bet they are going crazy."

"I shall arrive with my armada and a little surprise for everyone. See you soon." She clicked off with the flick of a finger. "A little...?" but the holoscan disappeared. He never got the question out.

Chapter Eight

The Birth of a Sender

Within their starship, the Elves continued their exploration. "Every point of agony is an uncompleted act of love. That's good. We can use that." Mefa was at the monitor board, ASTAR helping to instruct him on how to impact the grid.

The Elves had climbed back into my entire memory span and were now watching my father and me playing with the toys. It was Comcom who first realized: "Perhaps toys can be instruments that might impact the grid."

"But the grid itself has a history, so it will go back into the field," replied Mefa. "There will be information which will hold it in place." Finally, after a great deal of discussion, it was Misty who asked, "Can you go back in history and find what affected the grid the most?"

"Hmmm," mused Mefa. "Try about 1,482 years ago, in the little town of Bethlehem, where a baby Sender was born. His life seemed to have been a seeding of great love." The hologram showed the cloud narrowing dramatically like the neck of a bottle and then expanding out again after a few hundred years. "It had the greatest impact on the Grid of Agony. There must be something we can learn," said Mefa.

"It looks like he was born December 24, around midnight," said Comcom. "Let's travel to this place." "We'll be ready in a moment," was all Solah said, and then "Bethlehem, here we go." The starship disappeared into a swirl of light.

At the jarring motion, I awoke to find ASTAR trying to locate the little town. "What's happening?" I wondered out loud. Misty came over and placed her hand upon my chest. I was still on my back under the scanner. "We have come to look," was all she said. I was still a bit sleepy, but I sat up and watched. We wandered around the sky a little, looking down at various huts and little shelters. The hills were rocky, so there was little grass and no trees. "How could a Sender be born in such a place as this?" Mefa asked to no one in particular.

"Ha! Senders like to be born in places like this!" Comcom said. "They thrive on starting from nothing and embracing everything."

Finally, a little group of huts was found, with one containing a shelter for animals and a sleeping room for guests. From our position above the little town, ASTAR found the couple. She was heavy with child, lying in a manger, amidst a fresh pile of straw. "She is about to deliver," ASTAR reported.

Suddenly, across the sky from the direction of the small city of Jerusalem, a dark cloud arose. It came like a mass of darkness, much like a gathering storm. Misty was the first to sound the alarm. "Delovian shadow approaching. All alert."

ASTAR confirmed: "Delovian anti-matter: am sending photon storm to neutralize. It's beginning to dissipate, but it nearly reached the mother."

"We don't know what else they may be planning," said Comcom. "Let's take action. If they destroy this child before his time, it will be sad news for Earth."

Immediately, the Elves formed a circle and placed their heads into the ASTAR monitor. An orchestration of music, the harmonics of which I had never heard, sounded like a forest full of birds and angels singing in perfect harmony. It was the waves of the ocean and the winds of the sky, the roar of mountain streams and the rustle of a thousand leaves all in unison, filling the air, spilling out and covering everything. Like the voices of a thousand angels, it penetrated the fields, the flocks and the huts and rang across the hillsides. It was the music of life itself!

A great cathedral of light formed around the manger, covering the little village and the surrounding hills. It could not be penetrated, even by the darkness of the storm front that dissolved as soon as it touched the light. The darkness, like some great beast from outer space, raged around the light. It stormed and battered against it. Then, penetrating lasers of light swept into the cloud, cracking it, absorbing and dissolving it. Its power began to weaken and little whirlpools of darkness split off only to be zapped by another beam of light and completely dissolved.

On the defensive, the dark whirling little tornadoes sought to hide themselves only to be found by the light. Finally, the sky cleared. The Elves pulled back into the starship, all smiles. "Nothing like a little music to brighten up the night," smirked Mefa.

In the palace at the center of the city of Jerusalem, one dark form hid within the chambers of the king. Sensing his open snoring mouth, it entered. No one noticed.

Mary had raised herself up to a squatting position, which allowed her to help the baby to use the power of gravity to make his passage easier. Taken completely by her labor pains, she held to the railing pole above her head. Breathing steadily between the pains, she cried out and began to push. Breathing, pushing, breathing and pushing. With Joseph at her side, she could sense that the baby had started to come quickly. Filled with such love, the natural harmonics between mother and the child had taken over. At exactly midnight, the child was born.

Joseph helped the child enter the world. Covered with sweat from her ordeal, Mary lay back and took the child from the hands of Joseph, washed him gently and placed him upon her breast. She looked deeply into his eyes.

Back in the starship, Comcom observed, "The resonating frequencies of that baby and his mother are perfect frequencies of love."

"It is no wonder the world loved him," said Misty. "Look at the harmony of his intelligence. It is so comprehensive and unconditionally loving. He is the Master Sender."

"Look at how the planets are all aligned," pointed out Doray. "In fact, the galaxies are aligned. This is a truly intergalactic event."

"They are the most intricate harmonics of life I have ever recorded," said ASTAR. "Look," Comcom continued, "if we can align with this same frequency, we may be able to seed it into the Grid of Agony."

"The best time would be his time of birth," suggested Misty. And so it was that on the evening of December 24, at exactly 12 midnight, when the planets and the galaxies had all aligned in perfect harmony, the time was set for penetrating the matrix of the Grid of Agony. This magical moment became our entry point for the most amazing journey ever taken in human history.

"We have recorded the frequencies of love," reported Doray, "exactly as resonated from the child." Then he stood and faced his companions. I heard him say: "This one point in time, on the evening he was born, there occurred an alignment — a harmonic point at which even the hardest heart of the priest might be softened to its maximum listening power. This is a point at which all human beings who are caught in the Grid of Agony can find a way out." He was silent for a moment as everyone seemed to absorb what he was saying. He continued: "This is a point of time in which the field is most susceptible. It is the eve of the birth of Christ. At this time, the collective community is softened. It is a time when people care the most. This shall be known as Christmas Eve."

We all sat in awe of the moment. What a gift of life had just occurred. Then, after awhile, Comcom broke in: "OK we have our entry point. Let's get them out of here."

Then, everything swung back into action. "The powers of darkness are gathering in Jerusalem. ASTAR, where can we take them that they will be safe?" Misty asked. After a moment, ASTAR replied, "To Egypt. There is a safe oasis just across the desert. There they will be safe."

"Let it be done," commanded Comcom, and the starship swept down to the manger. "We must have a human carrier," said Doray. "We cannot do it ourselves," confirmed Mefa. "I know, I know," barked back Comcom. "Galactic prime-directive. How can we afford to keep the prime directives when the Delovians don't?"

"Don't ask me. I don't make the rules; I just play with them," smiled Doray. Then, after a brief moment he exclaimed, "We will use Nicholas!" "Yes," sighed Misty, "but how can we free him up from his trauma?"

"All he has to do is invite them to come!" barked Comcom. And so it was that I, at the tender age of six years, walked down the starship ramp and into the manger. "You must come," I said. Bless them both, for they immediately rose, picked up their few things and entered the starship. Such love emanated from them and from their baby — such intelligence as they looked around the starship at its strange yet beautiful shapes and colors and the little Elves who so tenderly tended them. They gasped as we lifted from the grounds of the inn and into the air. They were amazed at the lights and the sights of the starship. In almost no time, however, we arrived at the oasis. "We will be fine here," Mary said, as she descended the ramp. "Thank you," said Joseph. "Yes," she said, "Thank you — and from him as well." The little infant looked directly at me as his parents turned and walked toward the grove of trees.

"Well, that worked," exclaimed Tedo. The Elves were excited. In a moment, we were once again traveling back to my time and to the cave.

Chapter Nine

The Rebirth of a Sender

Misty looked at the belt buckle. I was, once again, asleep on the holoscan. "We must have a vehicle," she said, "some *form* around which he can rebuild his trust in life." Mefa took the buckle from her. He turned it carefully in his three-fingered hand and held it inside of the holoscan. "ASTAR," he motioned, "see if you can project something from this object that might give us a key to unlock this mystery."

Eight tiny reindeer formed inside the holoscan. Then the little red sleigh, so carefully crafted by Hans Claus, appeared. Suddenly, Doray swung over and joined in the search. "This has possibilities," he remarked, as Solah reached in and made a few adjustments. Toys began to form, filling much of the remaining space. Then Misty reached in. She took the frequencies of love that ASTAR had recorded from the birth in Bethlehem, and asked, "ASTAR, can we infuse these frequencies into the toys?"

"I will attempt it," replied ASTAR. A field of light arose surrounding the toys. Each toy seemed to glow with a faint light and then ASTAR reported: "I believe it was easier than I anticipated. That field is very strong."

"Sure enough," replied Misty. "With these toys, Nicholas may be able to send this frequency into anyone who touches a toy!"

"I wonder," broke in Comcom, "if this frequency will affect his personal field?" "Oh," said Misty, "will it be able to break the hold the grid has upon him?" They all looked at me. "I don't care," was all I said as I laid down, over exhausted from my travails and too tired to figure everything out.

"It may be possible," suggested Mefa, "that Nicholas' field dynamics will be impacted in a maximum way if we use his toys."

"And," continued Misty, "it may be amplified if we can produce a magic sleigh with eight tiny reindeer."

Doray pulled Comcom aside; "What shall we use for reindeer? We have auditioned different life forms to pull the sleigh. Birds, horses, elephants, crocodiles, giraffes, all types of animals want the job."

"I think snow deer would be best," suggested Misty. "I keep hearing snow deer from the mind of Nicholas." With a wave of her hand, Misty pulled up the answer I gave to my father:

"Maybe we could get some snow deer to pull us up."

"How many would it take?" The words of my father rang clear and true as Misty played them back.

"Eight." Misty replayed the words on the holoscan again. "Eight… Eight." She replayed it several times. "We should stay as closely as possible to his own creative imagination. He will accept the reality of what we are creating much easier then."

"OK. But what can we use for the snow deer?" asked Doray.

Together, the Elves scanned the Earth looking for deer of all types. "The caribou in the north are the closest we can find but they lack the desire to fly." Doray was having a struggle solving the snow deer problem. Then, over in the corner, Misty and Mefa had their heads together and she giggled.

"It will take a combination of genetic engineering to do this," suggests Mefa. "Let's check one more thing," Misty mused. "Here it is." She replayed Nicholas' final escape from the pit of hell.

"Then I could fly," said the Griff. "Then I could fly...fly...fly."

Doray immediately picked up the idea and followed through with the entire scene from the pits of hell of the monastery. "They want to fly." "And be free to play," he mused. "Do you think it might be possible?"

"It will take some fancy genetic engineering," warned Comcom.

"Every problem is caused by its solution," countered Misty.

"Let's do it!" commanded Comcom. In a moment, ASTAR hovered over the spring. Misty and Comcom approached the spring. "I don't like water. I had a bath about two hundred years ago and I don't need another one for another two hundred years," mumbled Comcom.

"Oh hush!" whispered Misty. "The water is warm and you won't dissolve. Now hold your breath and let's get on with creating his dream."

"Hold my breath? What do you think I am, human? I don't need to hold my breath. I can breathe water if I want to. See. Ha, Ha. I guess another bath won't hurt me," he said.

Comcom and Misty entered the portal beneath the wall of the monastery into the pits of hell where they knew the griffs were imprisoned. The volcanic light, the bubbling sulfur springs and the eerie sounds mingle with the shadows of darkness. "It is dangerously out of harmony here."

"It feels like a Delovian field — entropy everywhere — like the beginning of a black hole," he continued. "It is evil. Look, even the volcano acts unstable at our presence."

As they climbed out of the pool, a great rushing began from the depths of the lava bed and the walls of the caverns. "It's the souls of the damned," cautioned Misty. They paused as they watched the mystic images rise to the surface with great moaning sounds and anguish contortions. The Elves hesitated, unsure for a moment as to what to do when faced with such overwhelming powers of darkness.

"Unreal time," suggested Comcom. "It makes things so difficult." The Griff awakened by the sound of voices. It arose from its slumber and cast its great head over in the direction of the Elves. Spotting the two, it flapped its muted wings and angrily sounded a shrill scream. Before the Elves could respond, it attacked.

Seeing its intent, Comcom fumbled around in his pockets for something while Misty lifted herself with the levitator into the air. The Griffs began to assemble around them and, seeing her floating in the air, began to snap at her, roaring their disapproval. Finally, after what seemed like a long time to Misty, Comcom brought out a small set of chimes that he rang. No sooner had the chimes sounded than the Griffs calmed. Chaos ruled. Finally, the mother Griff roared. As a body the Griffs stopped. Stillness filled the cavern. The mother Griff lowered her head, her eyes curious. Comcom, still dripping wet, approached her slowly and signaled he wished to communicate.

The Griff dropped her head allowing Comcom to place his middle finger on her forehead so they could communicate. "We have come in the name of the Sender Nicholas," he said.

"Oh! The Sender! Well why didn't you say so?" She paused and dropped her head sending a message to her brood. All the griffs stretched their necks so their heads formed a circle around the Elves. "He is well?" she asked.

"He is traumatized by the powers of entropy but he is alive," misty said. He mentioned you might be willing to fly with him." She was a very good negotiator, so Comcom let her take the lead.

"We come from a world of flying dragons," said the Griff. "But we have been captured here for hundreds of years. I do not think I can fly anymore. My wings have become muted."

"Yes, the Sender told us that," answered Misty. "We would have to change your form. Are you interested?" She waited for an answer.

"Will it get us out of here and allow us to fly?" asked the Griff.

It was Comcom who responded. "Forever," he said. "You will be time-traveling."

"Did you hear my children? The Sender has called us to freedom," said the Griff. 'He chooses us to lead the way. We are free, we are free. We will be able to fly through all time."

"But Mother," cried the youngest Griff. "I can't fly. My wings are too short."

The Griffs all raised their heads and looked at Comcom. "Misty will explain it to you," he said with a bow and a wave of his arm as he pointed at Misty.

"You will go through a metamorphosis, a change of cell structure. I am afraid you won't be able to be big and fearsome dragons anymore," she explained. "We will have to change your form."

"What will we become?" asked another Griff.

"The best the Sender can do is to make you flying Reindeer," Misty replied.

"But reindeer don't know how to fly!" challenged the mother Griff. "They soon will if you will agree," Misty said.

Above them, high on the cavern wall and hidden in the shadows, a door swung silently open. A priest, dressed in black shuffled silently onto the balcony overlooking the pits of Hell. He heard the voices and his vision was drawn to the little circle of griffs. As they were conversing, the priest suddenly realized there were two people at the center of the circle. Immediately, he slipped back out of the cavern.

It was only a moment before almost the entire monastery was aware that intruders had entered their stronghold. Dwarg was rushing down to the balcony and hundreds of priests prepared torches and spears to confront the intruders.

"We griffs are the last of our species," the mother griff reflected. "Our galaxy was eaten by the Delovian black hole. We escaped because we were trapped in time here on Earth but we were also trapped in this monastery." She hung her head, recalling the sorrow she felt at her great loss.

"We can no longer reproduce," she continued. "We want to be free. Can you create new bodies for us so we can live in this world and fly through time freeing the lost souls who are caught in the Grid of Agony?" She looked down at these two small Elves, with eyes imploring some solution.

Comcom paused only for a moment. "We must enter your past and change your genetic codes," he said. "If you know how to enter our past and change our genetic codes, we will do it!" she said with finality. Then she raised her head and said, "Isn't that right my children?" As one, they replied: "Yes!"

"Can we do it before the priests completely surround us?" she asked. Comcom and Misty looked up and saw, much to their dismay, several hundred priests, all in black, creeping silently through the great cavern, slowly surrounding them.

"ASTAR," cried Misty, "program transport at your earliest convenience."

"No problem my friends. I will have you all out of there before you can say Merry Christmas," he replied.

Misty heard the override from Doray. "You must go now!" he told her telepathically. She looked upon the room, which was quickly filling with priests brandishing great clubs, torches and long sticks and becoming a battleground as they attacked their little party.

The griffs roared their disapproval. Throwing their wings out and snapping their jaws, whipping their tails back and forth, they attempted to drive the priests back. The priests thrust spears at them and, as the battle cry was raised, in the midst of its madness, Comcom sounded his chimes. Their special harmonic filled the room, bounced off the walls and reverberated back and forth. The sound echoed in the ears of the priests. They became confused, bewildered and then, as if by magic, the griffs and the Elves were wrapped in light.

Misty sent a message to the ship: "Implant the genetic code now." The griffs rose above the floor of the pit, the light weaving around them faster and faster. They seemed to dissolve themselves into eight little balls of light that formed an impenetrable shield around the Elves. The eight energized light-balls lined up two by two and pulled the Elves down into the water and out through the passage.

They were all transported immediately into ASTAR and before Dwarg could activate his anti-gravitational field, the starship whisked them away.

"ASTAR, can you help us transform each griff into the appropriate species?" asked Misty as they approached the crystal cave.

"Not a problem," he replied. The program was prepared as soon as I got samples of their blood." Doray looked down and there, on the floor, was a small trail of multicolored blood from the dragons.

Misty began to administer to their wounds. "You poor things," she purred. "You were so brave."

"You do not know the half of it," said one of the griffs.

One by one each griff, now a pulsating ball of light, transformed into a tiny reindeer. "It will be wonderful to fly once more," the mother said.

"You can remember when you knew how to fly?" asked Comcom.

"Oh yes. And much more!" she exclaimed. Her excitement growing as each of her children were transformed.

"Much more?" Comcom asked.

"Yes. We escaped the black hole's consummation of our own Galaxy. We are the only survivors that I know of because we were on a mission in another time zone when it occurred. When we returned we were almost swallowed by the blackness, but we escaped."

"Do you know about the black hole?" Misty asked. "What it is like?"

"Yes," replied the Griff. "We have been into its center. We were able to escape through a tractor beam latched to a seed crystal in another time. That is how we ended up in the Black Stone Monastery. The tractor beam was anchored in this space and time. We were drawn into the vortex of the black crystal, where we were enslaved by the crystal, and used to feed the fear of the people so the Grid of Agony would grow. Now that we are freed, we would like to serve to undo the harm we have created."

Her intent was so clear everyone cheered. "It can be done, it can be done." The Elves danced around the floor jubilant.

"What can be done?" asked the griff.

"Well, it's not done yet. Let's go to work!" said Mefa.

"The genetic code can be sculpted, for one thing," Mefa commented, as he twirled his finger in the holoscan. "We can certainly change the past." The balls of light spun around the bridge of the starship. Amidst the excitement, Comcom cautioned, "But only within certain boundary conditions."

Everyone could hear, but no words were being said: "We must always match the change with the will; the change must reflect the real intent of those being changed." The Griffs did not seem to care. They were so excited, they just wanted it done.

"That's right!" said Doray telepathically. "If the griffs did not want to be freed and to fly, we never could have made the change."

Everyone was busy. I slept.

Doray continued: "To impact the grid, humans must want to love. They must want to be Senders of love."

"Of course they do," piped up Tedo. "Everybody does."

Mefa was so involved it took a moment for him to respond. "Well, we all sure hope so," he said. "But that is why they bury the bad guys 10 feet deep." "What are you talking about?" asked Tedo. "They bury the bad guys ten feet deep because, down deep, everybody is good." He laughed as Tedo threw his cap at him.

"We can try it on Nicholas," said Misty. "He is a Sender. He could start this whole thing."

She paused a moment. "If we can get past this iron agony around his heart," she added.

"The toys should help," put in Tedo. "Let's take a look at putting the toys that are infused with the frequency of love into an action plan."

"Right!" Comcom almost shouted. "We need to decide where to make our first entry place?"

"Let's do the future," said Misty. Comcom looked at her. It was as if she could sense those dimensions that would require the most effort and those that would do the most good. He nodded his head in recognition. Such a love flowed between them, such a history of knowing, loving and working together.

A discussion ensued. Later it became known as "the great discussion." The Elves and the griffs began to explore every possible entry point. Doray used the images of my memory of my father's toys to re-create them. All the Elves pitched in. They created my little red sleigh, along with my little people dolls, boats and kites; the dancing children with the music toy; the puffer; discus; and even the musketeer who collected lightning. They talked and sang and danced as they worked and, finally, they created a big bag to hold all the toys so they wouldn't fall out of the sled.

"Now," said Misty, "any Sender can reproduce the love frequency of the Master Sender." All eyes turned to her. "All that is needed is for the Sender to imagine the Master Sender. His love will flood their being."

"But how does he get that frequency into the toy?" asked Mefa.

"It is quite easy," she replied. The Sender simply imagines a Place of Peace. He uses his senses and brings himself fully into the vibration of peace."

"That's it? It sounds too simple," retorted Solah.

"I am not finished" retorted Mefa. "The Senders imagine their own essence, their fullest potential self, in their Place of Peace."

"Do humans know how to do that?" asked Tedo. The Elves were caught completely into the plan.

"Senders do," she replied. "Once they are conscious of the Sender within, they simply align with their inner Sender. From there the inner Sender guides them to the Master Sender." Misty was confident her vision would work. It seemed so simple, so logical and so real that she did not fathom any doubts.

"So, once in tune with the Master Sender, then what?" asked Mefa.

"The Master Sender's harmonious love frequencies join with the Sender," joined in Comcom.

"And?" asked Tedo?

"All he has to do is hug a toy and it will receive those frequencies and pass them on to anyone who hugs the toy," concluded Misty.

"As soon as the toy is touched, it activates the love frequency," repeated Comcom. "The person will feel the spirit of love."

"I get it! I get it!" cried Doray. The Elves listened. "Anyone who is a Sender creates a real energy vibration coming out of each toy. It is like a tuning fork. Their love creates a single harmonic that reflects all the harmonics involved with love and then they get every toy in touch with that harmonic, like the chime that has been guiding Nicholas."

All the Elves smiled. Misty checked each toy. "It is time to awaken Nicholas," she calmly stated.

Mefa and Solah had been creating some dolls so the girls would have toys also. While they added the dolls to the bag, Doray continued to monitor the grid. We can line up the entry point on a vertical axis throughout parallel dimensions of time — including the past and future," he reported.

"Wait one more minute before we wake him up," said Comcom. "There are times of great agonies within the grid. Perhaps we should lock into a time coordinate before he awakens so we can just send him there."

"I want to be with him," said Misty.

"I also shall go," reassured Comcom.

"The rest of us will monitor the field and measure your impact upon the grid," offered Doray. "One more check. I want to look in on our life crystal."

Comcom disappeared through the portal. "If only we had the crystal we could travel to any dimension," he mused.

"What if the Delovians discover the crystal?" asked Tedo.

"They already have," Misty commented. Tedo looked at her and she only smiled. "They already know about it. They have already made a direct attack on it. But they cannot do it again. We are ready," she said.

But Doray replied, "They will get their human dupes to do it."

"We will keep a sharp outlook," she replied. "And let us hope the sleigh flies."

"If we had to get out of here, there would be no way to move the life crystal, she continued. "The cave contains the vortex coordinates for the crystal rejuvenator. It's one of the nerve centers for the entire planet. It's not transportable." They all knew she was right. "Let's hope we never have to leave."

Misty was keeping track of the converging powers of the inquisition. She could see them enter the valley of my father. "They're certainly ambitious — not a direct threat yet but definitely a growing power in growing the Grid of Agony," she said.

Meanwhile, at the sight of my burned-out home, the inquisitors sifted through the ashes, making sure that all the satanic devices were destroyed. Malevolent, peering through the crystal, somehow found my footprints in the ashes of the forest. "Follow me," he commanded Benton. The rest of the priests followed Benton's wave of his arm, as they headed through the charred forest up the crest in the direction of the elfin cave.

Looking into the crystal, Malevolent could see the cave. Gradually, as he drew nearer, the inside of the cave became clear. He could see the starship and, while he was mystified at seeing no one but children in the cave, he was confident that his faithful servants could handle the whelps. He picked up the pace, intent now upon the cave.

The Elves had completed the sleigh and the toys. Mefa had just completed the genetic engineering on the Griffs. "In order make this transformation, we will need to splice back into the entire history of their civilization. It's a coordinated event," he said.

As he ran the genetic records back through ASTAR's library, ASTAR interrupted, "Sir? I think you should look at this." As Doray drew nearer to look, the holoscan revealed a giant black hole eating the entire galaxy from which the griffs originated. A horrendous scene of great battles, of armadas beyond anything the Elves ever dreamed were possible, amassed against a very sophisticated galactic network composed of griffins and many other time-traveling peoples.

"There was no escape. No matter what they did, the Black Hole just consumed them all," Comcom said as he turned away.

"Their anti-matter neutrons absorbed everything they could throw at them. Look at those armadas. If they threw that at this galaxy, we would be eaten alive," gasped Tedo. "But these eight escaped. I wonder how. ASTAR, can you find out?"

Almost instantly, the griffs time jump was monitored. "They time warped out of their galaxy," reported Doray.

"But how would they have any reference?" asked Misty. "We used the black crystal," the Griff said. "That's why we were enslaved. We went right through the Black Hole and came out in a seed crystal time, here on Earth."

Then, he concluded, "Their next target!" The energy ball diminished a little until Comcom broke in. "Neatly done!" he exclaimed and the energy came back. The ball lightened again.

"This information must be shared with the Galactic Council," Comcom suggested. "Is there anything lost if we do the genetic shape shuffle?"

Doray was quick to respond: "Not that we can tell."

"OK. Everyone ready?" Comcom asked. They all nodded. "Let's do it."

Eight orbs of light swirled inward, down into the vastness of smallness, seeming to disappear when, almost as quickly, they began once again to form into shape. "Once the form is placed upon the quantum field of potential," Doray was saying, "all holographic matter will take whatever form is provided. We have just provided it with the form from Nicholas' fantasy. Suddenly! Eight tiny reindeer that can fly!"

In that same moment, the eight reindeer crowded the Starship. "Please!" interrupted ASTAR. "Perhaps outside?" They all smiled and opened the portal but, much to everyone's delight, the reindeer simply flew right through the sides of the ASTAR craft.

"Wonderful!" cried Mefa. "It worked!"

The reindeer were fitted with harnesses. A special set of levitation crystals was placed on each side of each reindeer so that they set up an anti-gravitational field set into the bottom of the sleigh. "The ability to change form also goes with it but it will last only a few seconds."

At Doray's raised eyebrows, ASTAR explained, "It allows them all to go through walls. They can deliver toys anywhere they want."

"Nice touch," commented Mefa. Everyone was smiling.

Comcom took over: "Now, in order to have a unified starter for the whole operation, we need some special chimes. These tiny bells are special. All Nicholas needs to do is jingle the bells and the sleigh will start."

At the jingle of the bells, I woke up. The Elves were all laughing. When I saw the sleigh and the eight tiny reindeer, the toys and the Elves, I thought at first I was in a dream. Then I thought the death of my father must have been the dream. I jumped down from the table and ran to the bag of toys. All my toys were there. "They weren't burnt! Ho! Ho! Ho!" I said out of pure delight.

"Actually, Nicholas," Misty gently suggested, "we created them for you from your memories."

"Oh, OHHH. Thank you. Thank you. Is my father here?" I asked.

"What we want you to do," she replied, "is to help us correct the death of your father. In order to do this, Nicholas, we need your help."

I was so overjoyed to see my toys that I hardly noticed the reindeer. "The priests are five minutes from the cave," reported ASTAR. "We must be ready."

"Not to worry," Comcom reassured us. "We are almost ready."

"Nicholas, give us a hand here," asked Misty. Together, they placed the bells on the harnesses. "It's to keep the harmonic," she said. "Here's your suit. It gets cold, you know, in between time."

My suit was red with a white collar. A black belt encircled it. I recognized the buckle. It was silver. I looked down at it and bent it forward so I could see what was written on the front. The name 'Santa' was inscribed upon it, with eight tiny reindeer pulling the sleigh.

"My father's gift!" I almost couldn't handle the memories and almost fainted, but the Elves rushed me through the process of getting me ready. Finally came the trimmings — the red hat with the white trim, the white gloves and the great black warm boots. I was ready.

"One minute. Board your sleigh, Santa." I was so excited. "Ho, Ho, Ho!" I tucked myself in with Misty and Comcom and the bag of toys. "Will it really fly?"

"Just jingle the bells," Comcom said.

Misty and Comcom had climbed in behind me. At that moment, shadowy figures could be seen creeping around in the cave. The priests of the Black Stone Monastery! I looked up at Doray. "Not to worry. We'll be gone in a second," he said. The portals of the starship closed and the cave took on a strange holographic effect. A granite crust grew over all the crystals! The life crystal looked like a big stone covered with dust.

"Where to?" I yelled as I slapped the reins and jingled the bells. The reindeer leapt into the air straight at the approaching priests. The quickness of their action caught the priests off-guard and they fell back in sudden panic. Dropping their clubs and spears they fumbled for their crosses. Before they could even think, we whisked beyond the cave and into the star lit sky. With a jolly "Ho! Ho! Ho!" and the jingle of bells, the little sleigh and its merry team twinkled out of sight.

The priests raised their eyes only to see the great starship whizzing overhead, all buzzing and flashing lights all around the cave. It hovered in the air above them. A great burst of air emitted from the bottom of the starship, covering them with dust. As they coughed, crawling to escape the cave, they could be seen jumping to their feet and running for their lives. The starship roared above them and then completely disappeared like a twinkle in the sky.

Malevolent, in the confusion and in his fright, had dropped the black crystal. As the dust settled in the cave, it covered the crystal. Slowly, after hours of hiding in the woods, Malevolent,

Benton and the priests crept up once again to the cave. They knew they could not return to Dwarg without the dark crystal. They must find it!

Chapter Ten

The Crack in the Cosmic Egg

I found myself, along with Misty and Comcom, in the cold zone, and it was a very good thing to have my warm red suit. The Elves did not seem to mind the cold. Just as suddenly, we popped out of the cold between times and found ourselves flying over a city of lights. It was the most beautiful thing I had ever seen — rows on rows of lights glowing into a horizon that seemed forever.

"Where are we?" I asked. Comcom and Misty were looking down into the small holoscan. "We are above a city of the future called Los Angeles." It is December 24, 2010."

"It's beautiful." Just then a great whooshing sound swept over us. The sleigh was thrown upside down and began to plummet toward the ground. But the reindeer quickly brought the sleigh back into balance. "Whoa!" I screamed. "What was that?"

"It was a flying cart called, I believe," said Comcom, "a jet." It almost collided with us," he said rather dryly. He continued as we all calmed down. "That's one of the toys of the future. It's called an airplane. People ride in them to get from one place to another. It is just like we are doing in this sleigh."

"Take us down closer," suggested Misty. "We don't want another one of those in our hair."

All I did was think about flying lower. It seemed that, upon my thought, the reindeer dropped the sleigh down just above the city. Comcom said, "Oh, oh; we overshot." He stuck his head into the holoscan. "ASTAR apologizes. He's doing a little adjusting on the controls. It has something to do with variations in the reindeer."

"Variations in the reindeer!?" Misty exclaimed. "So what are we supposed to do here? There probably isn't any agony in a place as beautiful as this." The reindeer just looked at each other and rolled their eyes. "Let's see if — somewhere — we can't find a little agony in L.A.," she suggested.

"Look. There's a spot right beneath us," said Comcom. "That didn't take long," I thought as the sleigh suddenly swooped downward. We circled above a dark alley between rows of large buildings and old houses.

"It's a little 5-year-old girl! Why, she's dying!" cried Misty.

"Let's get down there," said Comcom and we looped downward. The reindeer seemed to know just where to go. They dropped down into a little alleyway behind a large dilapidated house and an old building. At first it did not appear as though anyone was there.

"Checking," said Comcom.

"Yes. Right over there!" said Misty, pointing to a pile of rubble.

I stepped out of the sleigh. Reaching into my bag of toys, I found a little doll. It would be perfect for girls. Holding it to my heart, I allowed the light of the Master Sender to radiate through my heart and back into the doll. For a moment, the entire alleyway was lit with light. Softly, I stepped toward the little bundle of rags and tuff of hair I could see huddling amongst the trash.

"Ho, Ho, Ho!" I chuckled as two bright brown eyes peered out at me through a rumble of rags. The eyes, however, did not respond to my chuckle. In fact, they were vacant, empty, lonely beyond touching, resolved and almost dead. I was shocked to see a child so far removed from fun and life.

Kneeling beside her, I held out the doll. She did not respond. Ever so gently, I put the doll in front of her. There was still no response, so I lifted one of her hands. Her fingers were cold to my touch. I wondered if she might not be frozen or so near death we could not help her. Then, tucking the doll next to her heart, I found her other hand and placed both hands over the doll so she was, in effect, hugging the doll.

Still her eyes told me nothing. I waited, my heart filled with concern for this empty, lovely little creature who seemed so much a part of the trash, thrown away by the huge city. Suddenly, just as I was about to turn and ask Misty's advice, a faint glow appeared in her vacant eyes. From some inner void she flickered into realization for her eyes slowly turned downward to look at the doll. Little by little, her fingers seemed to encircle it and then her arms embraced it, holding it tight.

I sat on my heels beside her, watching the warmth come into her body. She rocked slowly back and forth, back and forth, the energy of life returning. The color of her cheeks took on a pinkish red glow and her lips began to lose their blueness. Her breathing deepened and suddenly she opened her eyes and looked right at me.

"Who are you?" she gurgled. I could see her eyes now open and absorbing. I looked at the doll. Her eyes followed mine. "Ho, Ho, Ho!" I giggled and, turning on my heel, I rose from beside her and walked to the sleigh.

"Wait," she called weakly, trying to get to her feet. But the reindeer were already geared to fly on their way. We twinkled out of there, although now I wish I had taken more time. I had never had friends of my own age and it would have been wonderful to have a friend. I knew, however, deep inside that it was all right and I never had time to think about it twice. I just jingled the bells and, with a "Ho, Ho, Ho!," we disappeared into the stars.

As soon as we entered the space-time continuum, the coldness hit me with a jar. It seemed much colder and, after a few seconds, it did not go away. It was so cold that everything started to freeze solid. I could hardly move and then slowly, I saw a bubble forming around the sleigh and the reindeer. It grew warmer and I turned around to find Misty and Comcom with their heads in the holoscan. "What's happening?" I shouted.

My voice reverberated around inside the bubble and I thought for a moment it might break. Comcom stuck his head out of the holoscan for a moment and said, "Don't shout. Be very still and focus. We have dropped through some sort of crack in the cosmic egg. Look!" He pointed with his long central finger and, through the bubble, I could see the open mouth of a great black hole.

We stood on the edge of the hole and appeared to be slowly circling inward. "Is it going to eat us?" I whispered.

"We hope not. Doray and ASTAR are still in touch with us but we are six galaxies away," he said.

"How did we get here?" I asked.

"We must have dropped through a crack in the field. The space-time continuum is cracked." I looked bewildered, and he said, "I'll explain it later. For now, hold on to that bag of toys."

I looked down and my toys seemed to take on a glow of their own. A light was pulsing through them, supporting the bubble. I held on and I got a little warmer just knowing that the frequency might still be with us.

Once the reindeer saw the black hole, they put their heads together. I could not tell what they were doing, so I just hung onto my toys. After a few seconds, Comcom pulled his head out and said to me, "Doray says it was a little gift from our Delovian brothers. They were monitoring our first flight and set a trap for us. They tried to send us all straight into the black hole."

"How do we get out of here? We are sinking more and more every second!" I almost shouted.

His next remark did not help at all. "The reindeer say that the only way out is in."

"What does that mean?" He did not answer because his head was back in the holoscan. Then, after a moment he pulled it out again. "It means we have to go through the black hole in order to find our way out."

"But nothing comes out of a black hole. Nothing ever comes out." I was perplexed, almost in panic. I could see that both Misty and Comcom were perplexed by the reindeer consensus.

As if in answer, from out of the rim of the black hole appeared an armada of thousands of shadow starships. They unfolded from behind a curtain of darkness, armed and ready for battle. Without warning, a pure black ball of anti-matter shot toward us. "Anti-matter in four seconds. More on the way" said the holoscan.

"How can we defend against it locked in time?" asked Comcom.

The reindeer dove beneath the ball and it sped by them harmlessly into empty space. "Whew, that was close," I breathed a heavy sigh. "More anti-matter coming," the holoscan reported, "in a pattern this time. Look!"

From three dark starships, each on the opposite sides of the sleigh, came a coordinated burst of blackness. It spread like a blanket, leaving us no room to maneuver. It filled the sky around us. The armada had situated itself in all directions and, without any discussion, was attempting to destroy every trace of our sleigh and valuable cargo.

As the first of the blanket of blackness hit against the bubble a blinding flash of light burst from the bubble and turned a blanket of light back onto the armada. Delpha, from her control ship, saw the light and screamed, "Shoot it! Neutralize it before it dissolves everything!"

The warships of the armada turned their anti-matter upon the light. The light absorbed their bombs of blackness until both the bombs and the light were used up. The three warships were completely destroyed in the process. It was clear that Delpha's starship would have been next.

"Idiots!" she shouted. "No more anti-matter bombs. Move in. Take them prisoner."

A thousand small fighting crafts took to the air from out of the larger ships of the armada. Like cockroaches in the night, they swarmed toward us in waves firing smaller beams of pulsating blackness in patterns that seemed impossible to dodge. The reindeer began to maneuver the bubble and sleigh as we darted among the ships of the armada. And dodge the reindeer did. "We cannot hold out forever!" Comcom observed.

Once in awhile a black beam would bounce off the bubble. Each time, in a crack of lightening, the black beam would be transformed into a light beam that would disintegrate whatever it touched by going back into the anti-matter source from the craft of the Delovians. Then, to our amazement, it would completely dissolve the craft.

Looking toward the reindeer, Comcom nodded his head and said, "They are good at this game." Then he paused a moment as the sleigh lurched strongly to the left, then up, then down. "It's how they escaped in the first place," I stammered through all the jostling.

Delpha was in a rage. "Get them, get them. What is the matter with you!? Have you lost your senses? It is just one little whatever pulled by some dumb animals. Get them!"

The smaller crafts could not however, capture the sleigh. The reindeer were able to dodge everything they tried. Even I knew, however, that we could not stay there for long. As long as the toys were in the bubble, we were safe because the frequency of the Master Sender somehow turned the anti-matter into universal energy. The flight patterns of the reindeer kept us from being captured.

"The longer we stay here, the further into the black hole we get dragged!" mumbled Comcom as he withdrew from the holoscan, looked around at where the sleigh was positioned, and then stuck his head back into the holoscan.

Suddenly, the sleigh lurched out of control. We plunged further into the mouth of the black hole. Whirling in a great circle, plunging ever downward, the armada pursued us, with Delpha shrieking her curses and pleasures at our every setback and her armada always ready to fire upon us. The light of stars above began to darken and the universe into which I was born, was slowly disappearing.

With Comcom's and Misty's heads in the holoscan, my arms around the bag of toys and the reindeer so actively directing our little sleigh, we appeared a desperately meager team against an opposition that swallowed whole galaxies.

I listened as Misty and Comcom talked in the holoscan. "Can you locate the cause of the fracture?" he asked.

"They set us up, monitoring every move we made," she replied. "They planned that crack and pulled the sleigh right into the mouth of their black hole."

"According to the reindeer, we need a seed to pull them back," she said.

He shook his head. "The only seed we have is the black crystal and that's in the hands of Dwarg."

Then Misty got an idea. "What about the life crystal?" she asked.

Comcom thought for a moment. "Maybe but we would need a Sender." We waited while he probed the holoscan. "Everything is shielded by the agony grid. To get through we would need a Sender whose love was greater than the grid."

Finally, through the holoscan, a voice, covered in static, broke through. "We... reach you! come..."

"It's Doray!" shouted Comcom. Then he and Misty did a very strange thing. They pulled out of the holoscan and held both their hands around its vortex. The message cleared.

"This is Doray. Where are you? We have been looking for hours!"

Without changing their position I could hear their telepathic message back to Doray. "We are on the edge of the black hole. It must have been a crack in the cosmic egg. Can you hook us up to the life crystal through a Sender?"

"Is there any way back?" asked Doray.

"We don't know" replied Comcom. "We are looking but the best plan is to use a reference beam to tune into."

The connection faded for a moment but, as we circled upward amongst the charging holons of the black armada, it came back again. "We must align the life crystal to the beam!" Comcom reiterated.

"It's broken!" Doray shouted back. "We are locked into the time-space continuum so what can we use?"

"The best thing would be a human carrier," Comcom shouted back. "Is there anyone?"

Silence followed, then "We only know of two. Yet... nah." Doray was unsure.

"What?" Comcom bleated out.

"It's what humans call a wild goose chase!" cried Doray.

"Tell me, there's no time to find him so what are you thinking?" demanded Comcom.

"Only the little girl." Everyone went silent. Doray continued, "She's the only one that received the frequency."

There was another moment of silence as the sleigh careened through a hailstorm of dark pellets. Then Comcom said, "It will depend on what she did with those love vibrations when Nicholas gave her that doll." Then, as though his mind were made up he shouted, "Tune in. Give her 15 years. See what you get. Remember, we will lose in real time the years in between so Nicholas will be older. Make it as soon as possible."

"OK. It's worth a shot." The communication was cut off and Misty and Comcom let go of their circled hands. "Hurry we have only half an hour before we freeze solid."

After a moment, Doray was back again. "We got her on the screen. She is teaching a classroom of handicapped children."

"Is there any way to tell if the love frequency took?" Misty asked. "The only thing is...yes. The doll is on her desk," Doray reported.

"Then hit her with the beam." Comcom commanded.

There was only one chance. We did not have time to track the little girl at the orphanage to see the next 15 years of her life. Nor was there time to test if the seed of love had grown strong enough to grow the strength of a Sender. Nor was there any way to test if she was strong enough to be the conduit for a powerful tractor beam, or whether she could hold the beam long enough to draw the sleigh back from the depths of darkness at the very entrance to the black hole. It would take profound love, strong love, as well as total and unconditional love, without contamination.

At the same time, something deep in me knew the black hole was a living thing. Quietly, so as to not disturb anyone, I reached in my bag and picked a toy. It was the silver discus my father made for me. I pushed it to the edge of the bubble and it slipped right through. I watched as it skimmed its way down into the very center of the funnel of the black hole.

"Comcom?" I turned to look at him and started to talk. "Can the frequency heal the crack in the cosmic egg…?" He looked at me as though he never expected me to have an original idea. Before he could say anything, I went on. "while we are here?" I paused.

He was thinking. "You mean fortify against the Delovian hoards and close the black hole?" he asked.

"Well," I said, "I just seeded the black hole with …the disc…" The sleigh was being thrown into great turbulence. I looked out and down into the black hole. "Let it collapse in on itself and see what happens… while we make our escape?"

Before I could point out what I saw happening down in the black hole, Doray's voice came back through the holoscan: "The Sender will have to stay in the vortex of love long enough for that sleigh to get back. You could do hyperspeed but every division of hyperspeed takes time from the life of Nicholas. He will age."

Comcom responded: "Still, we can't keep him out there at the speed of light because he would freeze long before he got back."

"Crystal might not be able to hold the beam for more than a few minutes," Doray said. "It's going to take an awful lot of love to make that work even if we use hyperspeed. If she fails or even if anyone who is not a Sender touches her, it will break the beam and you will be lost along the path."

Then Misty warned, "The crack in the cosmic egg is growing. The black hole is flowing through. We all may be doomed no matter whether we get back or not." I was looking down into the center of the black hole where the disc had flown. Great bolts of lightening, huge explosions of light and energy vortexes were bolting everywhere. The light was growing in size. Like a flash fire, it was spreading through the black hole and would soon be upon us.

"Comcom! Look!" I shouted.

He jerked his head out of the holoscan. "What?" he almost shouted back.

"Look." I pointed in the direction of the rising storm of light.

"What is it?" His face was wrinkled in a fierce glare.

"I think it's the disc with the love frequency," I beamed. His eyes went wide and he jammed his head back into the holoscan.

"We have got to get out of here now. Use the beam." I held my breath. What, I wondered, was to become of us?

In a run down section of the Maryland School District, in one of the numberless suburbs of Los Angeles, California, a young woman sat in the middle of a circle of special, handicapped children. She was unaware of the galactic events that were about to descend upon her.

"Warm," she said. "Warm. Feel the warm on your hands. Warm." She held her hands out in front of her palms facing together. "Can you feel the warm?"

The children acted as though they did not know she was even there but Crystal knew they knew. That is why the principal, Mr. Geoffrey, considered her such a gift to his school. Somehow the children trusted her and responded to her like no other he had ever seen.

She reached out and placed a little boy's palms so they were facing each other, a little ways apart. "Warm? Bradley, can you feel the warm?" Bradley glanced at her quickly so as to not reveal he understood yet there was a moment of connection. She smiled. It was not much compared to regular students but it was a monumental gesture from a special student. She filled with gratitude. Gently taking Bradley's hands, she held them over the little girl lying in fetal position in front of her. "Warm on Lynn?"

Pretending not to know, Bradley held his hand over Lynn. Crystal could feel the heat. Bradley had a special gift of healing and, almost immediately Lynn began to respond. She began to sit up and move toward Bradley.

"Good boy, Bradley!" Crystal clapped her hands.

Bradley clapped his hands liking the game. He knew little Lynn was very upset when she came into the class that morning, led by the nurse. He knew why, too. The nurse had slapped her when she wouldn't cooperate in getting dressed. Only the nurse didn't know that he knew.

Crystal understood his secret knowing and his ability to heal. She was teaching her handicapped and emotionally disturbed children how to heal one another and calm each other's emotions. Suddenly, without any warning, Bradley jumped up and took Lynn by the hand. "Warm!" he shouted. Not sure of what he was doing, Crystal hesitated. The other children, however, did not. They, too, jumped up and formed a circle around Crystal.

It was at that moment she was gripped by the sudden force of the tractor beam. As in a seizure, she fell to the floor barely able to breathe. For a split second she almost panicked in her worry for the children. Something in the flow lifted her, calming so deeply that she was flooded with a peace she had never known could exist. She let go of herself as every cell of her body, every ounce of blood and brain was flooded with a love so great she released her will completely to its unfolding.

As in a trance she reached out across what seemed like an endless space, past stars and galaxies, to a small red sleigh with eight tiny reindeer. In her heart of hearts she called to him, the little boy who had given her love and brought her back to life. "Come to me. Come to me," she called. The message seemed to float into space along a strange but wondrous beam, not of light alone, but of life itself, reaching outward, making contact. She released herself to its desire.

The children seemed to understand. They surrounded her with a circle of love, opening their arms and swaying to the love. At that moment, Mr. Geoffrey looked in through the window of the classroom door. He was about to pass on to the next class when he did a double take. He looked again and stared at the circle of children, swaying back and forth around the teacher who seemed to be having some kind of seizure. Immediately, he opened the door and rushed in to take control of the situation.

As he approached the circle, Bradley said, "NOO, NOO. DON'UCH! DON'UCH. WARM..." as he and the children held hands. Mr. Geoffrey was taken back by the fact that handicapped and emotionally disturbed children would not let go. Thinking they would let him pass, he made another attempt but they would not let him pass. Finally, becoming exasperated, he attempted to force his way through but the children threw themselves between him and their teacher. No matter what he did, they would not let him pass.

In desperation, he fled the room, ran to his office and dialed 911. "Mr. Geoffrey, Maryland Elementary School. Teacher down. Having some form of seizure," he gasped breathlessly. "Room 144. Come immediately."

"Please stay on the line," the woman on the other end of the phone requested. "Give me your name one more time. Is it Mr. ...?"

"Geoffrey! I am the principal. One of my teachers in having a seizure of some sort."

"And what is your address?" asked the voice on the phone. "It's Maryland Elementary School. 96555..." he stammered. "Yes, 9655..." He waited a moment. "96555 Macmillan Avenue."

"96555 Macmillan Avenue." The voice affirmed. "And where is the teacher located?"

Mr. Geoffrey was getting agitated. "Room 144. Come to the front door. My office is just to the right of the entry. I will guide your people from there. Hurry."

He went to hang up but the voice was emphatic. "Just stay with me, Mr. Geoffrey. I have already notified the ambulance and they are on their way. They should be there within four minutes. Now, does she have any known history of heart attacks or seizures?"

"No, not that I know of," he replied.

"Does she..." the woman continued, getting as much information as possible that might help the paramedics. Mr. Geoffrey was beside himself with worry.

"Look I really have to get to that class. They are handicapped and there is no one there to take charge of things..." Just when he was about to bolt, the ambulance drove up, sirens screaming. "Oh they are here. Thanks." He dropped the phone onto its hook.

"This way, gentlemen!" he shouted as he motioned the paramedics down the hallway to Crystal's classroom. "Room 144." Two men ran ahead with a respirator and some other equipment while another prepared to follow with a stretcher. As they burst through the door, the children were calm in their circle of love. They hardly seemed to notice the men as they burst into the room.

One of the paramedics rushed to the circle and tried to break through saying, "OK, kids, I'll take it from here." At his touch the children sprang into action. "NOOO. DON'UCH! DON'UCH!" screamed Bradley. The others formed a barrier, weaving back and forth, "Don'no no no no no no." They would not allow the men to touch her. Taking command the young paramedic picked up two of the children and tried to set them aside but they scrambled back and were joined by two more. He became rougher and more demanding. "Hey, you kids get out of here!" he shouted.

Mr. Geoffrey stepped up, "They are handicapped and don't know what you are saying."

Bradley looked sharply at Mr. Geoffrey. "No 'uch," screamed Bradley.

Then Mr. Geoffrey began to understand. "The children do not want us to touch her. They love her very much and think she is hurt."

"We are here to help her," said the young paramedic, more gently. Then, catching the eye of the Principal and the other paramedic, he knelt and hugged two of the brave children. Mr. Geoffrey held onto two more as the other paramedic rushed in to help the poor girl in the seizure. But the remaining children threw themselves into his path. He fell and almost stumbled on Crystal.

"NOOOO!" shouted Bradley. "Nooooo!" shouted the children. At that moment a sleigh driven by eight tiny reindeer appeared to swoop through the wall. It flew in a slow circle around the room and settled to the floor. It was crusted with ice and appeared as though everything was frozen through but, upon landing, the ice began to crack and fall off. First the reindeer stamped nervously to free themselves from the coldness of their shell. Then two Elfin figures slowly unraveled themselves from the back of the sleigh. I was the last one out. To my amazement, I was a full-grown man.

The principal and the paramedics were speechless. The children were jumping up and down for joy and clapping their hands. "Warm" said Bradley as he placed his hand on his heart.

Crystal had not yet recovered as I stepped from the sleigh. I was so taken by the fact my body was older, I could hardly stand. But I saw the woman who made our return from the edge of the black hole possible and I knelt beside her.

I reached down, lifted her head in my right hand, brushed a lock of her hair from off her sweating brow so it would be out of her eyes and looked deeply into her eyes. She had the most beautiful lavender eyes I had ever seen. I was not accustomed to women and I grew a little uncomfortable as her eyes opened even wider.

"You!" she gasped.

I kissed her then, on the forehead. "Thank you," I said, trying to find words for my profound gratitude.

"You did good."

I could not repress a gentle laugh. "Ho, ho, ho." It was more of a chuckle. Then I grew more serious.

"You did real good." It seemed I had known her forever. "I'll be back."

Still a little dazed, she sputtered, "But, but, who ARE you?" Misty and Comcom were in the sleigh. I knew we had only moments before the Delovian tracking would lead them to this room and to her.

"I must go. I'll be back."

She was up on her feet now. "Wait. I'm coming with you." But we were already gone. "See you December 25," I shouted back, not knowing if she heard. Suddenly we were back in the cave. ASTAR was there and the Elves poured out of the starship to greet us.

"There's a good chance that little trick you played with the discus has sealed the crack in the cosmic egg!" said Doray as he jumped up and gave me a hug. "You've grown some since we saw you last."

"How'd we get caught in that thing anyway?" I asked.

"They laid a trap for us," said Doray. "The council was not pleased. It appears as though they have been using the black hole to steal matter." "What can they do with matter?" I asked.

"Almost anything we can do with anti-matter. It's a way to take their wastes and transform them into pure energy," Doray explained. I must have looked a little perplexed, "Energy can be transformed into anything you want. All you have to do is put form around it and it becomes whatever you make it into."

"So, Delpha's armada?" I conjectured.

"They have been turning energy into war machines in order to get more energy," Comcom concluded.

"An old story," replied Misty, "and they are headed here!" All eyes turned to her.

"Delpha's armada! She's got something sinister. We must be prepared."

"But I thought you said we sealed up the crack," Mefa exclaimed.

"But she was on this side of it. She's trailing our tractor beam." Misty seemed to know. I thought she just might be right but I never ever even thought of such a thing.

Then Doray asked, "What has she got to gain? As soon as she hits any matter, she will lose more of her own energy. She'll soon be eaten up by matter."

"Not if she can draw on the Grid of Agony," said Solah. "The Grid of Agony is like a beacon to her. She will find her way to earth through the grid. It is the energy that gives the black crystal its power and sends out the message. It's like a death wish from planet Earth. She is simply answering it."

"So the entire armada is on its way to earth?" Doray asked.

"Yes. I am afraid it is," replied Misty.

Suddenly I was terribly discouraged. I just started thinking about how I had lost my mother to the inquisitors before I was old enough to remember. It seemed like yesterday that I had lost my father to them. I had then been almost lost to the black hole and now I had the weight of the world on my shoulders. I had even lost my childhood. I didn't know what could be done and I didn't feel like doing anything. I had no friends except the Elves, whom I loved dearly. But they were far beyond me in wisdom and power and I couldn't think as fast as they did. I was lonely for my own kind.

I withdrew to the far side of the cave. I was a grown man. They said I was 21 but I felt like I was still 6 years old. I didn't want to fight Delpha and her armada. I didn't want to fight anyone. I couldn't forget the children in the sweatshop in the Black Stone Monastery. They would all be dead or priests by now, which was the same thing. The old agony began seeping back into my body. I was even disgusted that it had returned.

"I'm going to see my place," I said, sort of out of the blue. Somehow, though, I felt I was resolved. The Elves offered no resistance. They seemed to understand. Misty came to me and, undoing her wrist levitator, placed it on my wrist.

"Remember," was all she said, but the look in her eyes told of a love that was forever. I turned away with tears in my eyes but my heart felt cold, like so much sorrow had passed my way in such a short time. I could not find myself. I knew I had to face the Grid of Agony for myself. As I was about to turn, Doray came to me.

"The Grid of Agony is everywhere. The inquisitors will be looking for Nicholas Claus. If you tell anyone who you are it will be reported and you will be immediately taken into custody. Do not let them get you because they surely want to kill you more than any other human."

"I will go in disguise. I will give myself a new name. I will call myself Kris. Kris Kringle. Oh by jingle, I am Kris Kringle," I laughed, trying to make light my heavy heart and to reassure them I would be all right."

They, of course, saw right through me. Comcom tried one more time. "The Grid of Agony can be diminished by acts of love. Toys can be infused with the love frequencies of the Master Sender and they can carry his love everywhere. Stay with us. Help us make such toys and deliver them to children of all ages. By seeding the Grid of Agony with the toys of love, we have hope that we can contain, even maybe end the grid, once and for all."

"But the grid is seeded by the black crystal. Why don't you just destroy the crystal?" I asked.

"We cannot. We are forbidden to do so and, if we tried, such a burst of blackness would occur, that it would surely speed Delpha's armada and the black hole right to earth. There would be no chance then. We are not allowed to intervene." His eyes were imploring me, almost begging me to listen.

"Well, it's my world and I can intervene," I said. They helped me pack. I took food and, donning a new set of warm clothes with an extra change in my pack, I turned to leave without a word. As I rounded the bend in the cave, I took one look back at my Elfin friends. They raised their hands as one in farewell to me. "I'll be back," is all I said.

"We'll be making toys," I heard Mefa say, but I was already picking up a fast jogging pace back to my home, which I knew was in ashes. It was the only home I knew. I was going to find my lost childhood. I looked down and noticed the belt buckle. I turned my sweater over it so no one else would even know it was there.

The Crack in the Cosmic Egg

Chapter Eleven

Kris Kringle and the Black Crystal

I am detached from my body. The pain has been so great for so long that I am no longer in my body but watching from outside, somehow aloof. I know I am near to death.

"Ha! Ha!" *I can hear the words of Dwarg spit into my face. "You, the mighty Sender! You, the sneaky Kris Kringle, making toys for children and teaching love. Bah! You are nothing and all your work is now turned into agony. Yes! All those precious little minds you tried to save have been put into the sweat shops. You thought you'd be so clever as to sneak in here and grab the crystal a second time. Ha! Ha! But we caught you, didn't we! And look at you now. Not much left. You are almost completely ours, your soul turned over to the black force! The Grid of Agony has consumed you, Sender!"*

My mind tumbled down, down, down into the blackness. Then I remembered:

I was sifting through the ashes of my home. The sadness of loss and the misery of loneliness caused a great agony to come upon me. I had no one to call my own. Trapped in the body of a young man but missing my years from 6 to 21. How can a man make up for that?

I stayed several days and made a crude shelter under a new dense growth of pine trees. I was hidden and filled with nothing but memories of this place. It took but a couple of days until my growling hungry stomach reminded me that a man cannot live on his memories. I must strike out and find out for myself who I am and what kind of man I am.

I headed south and east, toward the village of Milan. I had no one I knew and no friends or anyone to help me. I had no money but only the strength of my own arm and the use of my own brain to make my way. I knew the peril the world was in and how short my time might be, and yet I could say nothing to anyone about it. I could only take my stand and make my own way.

My mind kept repeating itself. My heart was cold within me. I had lost myself, my sense of being. I knew not who I was or where I was to go. Yet, deep within me, someone walked with me, but through my cloud I could not see or feel but only sense a presence.

Survival took hold of me. It snowed and I, huddled under my little shelter, almost froze. Finally, after two days of whittling under the tree, I could stand it no longer. I left my meager shelter and walked into the storm took the carvings I had made and stuffed them into a pocket inside my wrap. For a full day and a night I walked through blinding snow until, at last, I dropped down beneath the snow line. From there I was caught in a steady rain. Soaked to the skin and shivering with cold that snatched away my strength with every step, I finally stumbled into the yard of a little mountain dwelling.

With barely enough strength to knock, I sagged against the door. I heard the latch and staggered to gain my footing. The door opened just a crack and I looked down into two big doe eyes that belonged to a little girl. "What do you want?" she asked in a voice that held little caring.

"I am freezing and I need a little warmth. Can you let me in until I dry out and get warm? I won't be any trouble." I don't remember anything after that except that I woke up the next morning beside the fireplace. I was wrapped in a warm comforter and my clothes had been removed and had dried beside the fire. A pot of porridge sat steaming on the table. I didn't turn over or make a sound but watched the little girl as she set the table. "You can stop pretending. I know you are awake. Get dressed," she said almost as if she were my mother.

I grabbed my pants and pulled them under the comforter. "You'd best be gone when Grantz gets back." "Who's Grantz?" I almost stuttered. "He's my owner. He don't take kindly to strangers." She was very matter-of-fact about it. I finished dressing in silence. "Thanks for taking me in. I was almost a goner."

"I shouldn't of done it. There'll be hell to pay if he finds out." She turned and placed a bit of bread on the table.

"Sorry to be trouble." Remembering the carvings I had made, I reached inside my coat and pulled out a carving of a woman holding a child. "What's your name?" I asked. "My name is Abbey but my owner calls me every name but that."

"Well, I want to thank you, Abbey. You have a good heart and someday you will be a wonderful mother."

I handed her the carving. She looked at it and her eyes widened. I doubt she had ever been treated with kindness from the way she looked at the carving, turning it over and over in her hands. "For me?" she asked.

I nodded "Yes."

For a moment, I thought that she would cry but she quickly composed herself, got up from the table and put the carving under the bedding in her corner of the room. "You better eat and run. Grantz will be back soon." I could see the fear in her eyes. I quickly ate, thanked her again and slipped out into the early morning sunshine.

As I was coming down out of the woods, I saw a large man climbing the grade across the stream. He was bearded and overweight and carried a large pack upon his back. "It must be Grantz," I thought to myself.

I awake to water. Someone has thrown water over me. Benton picks me up one last time and secures me to the rack. I am so weak, I am near the last of my inner strength. My physical strength was gone long ago.

"You are a tough one," he says. "I'll give you that. But there's not much left of you now. It's time for you to pass on to the depths of hell where you and all your kind belong."

"Hell could probably use a few toys," I mumble. He tightens the wristbands with a jerk. "You know why I woke you up rather than just tearing you apart?" he growls.

"Why? Have some pleasant thoughts you wanted to share with your only friend?" I managed a weak smile.

"Because Dwarg says God has a special surprise for the wicked. It will be here soon. I wanted you to know it was coming because you won't be here to get it."

Unknown to me, the Elves were monitoring my experience on the rack. I let my mind go. As in a dream, I could hear: "He is nearly finished. We must bring him back. Hang on, Nicholas. We are almost there." It was Misty. Ah, my Misty. The only real friend I ever had who played with me. Here I am all tied up, I joked to myself, and no one to play with except Benton. And he, at that moment, brought me back to a pain so deep that I blacked out for a moment.

I am haunted by memories of children who are unloved, abused and used: children in the sweatshops of the Black Stone Monastery and in the towns, who had no toys, no one to love them, no one to play with and all they knew was work from dawn to dusk. They were beaten and always hungry. No one cared for them. No one gave them clothes or warmth. In each town, the enforcers and the priests punished anyone who was kind to children. Many children died and their mothers and fathers could or would do nothing about it.

I remember going down the mountain and into the valley below. In my darkness, it seemed that everywhere I went it was the same. Still, everywhere I went I made carvings. They were little toys and I always infused them with love. I do not know if it made any difference but I know it seemed to make the children feel better at least for a moment. The Grid of Agony was so widespread that my own heart could not shake off the oppressive sadness I felt for their suffering. I could not tell if my love for them was any advantage to anyone, but still I trudged on looking for what I could not tell, knowing I must go on until I found it. Lost was my own childhood. Without parents, without friends, without family, I trudged on and on. Deeper and deeper I slipped into the matrix of the Grid of Agony.

The priests in power laughed at me. "A worthless soul," they scowled. Each enforcer looked upon me with absolute suspicion and often I was cast into the jailhouse to please their whims. I did not resist and so I was imprisoned and then let go to wander to another town. In one of those nameless towns, I overheard a conversation between two priests.

"Malevolent said the Savior is coming soon," said one.

"Does he know when?" asked the other.

"It will be soon now but no one knows for sure."

"What will happen when he comes?"

"The evil of the world will be completely destroyed. All the wicked will die. Those who serve the source will be lifted up to heaven," said the priest.

It came to me then, as I huddled in the shadows listening to their hopes, that the "source" was the dark crystal. "She will use the seed to draw them here." It dawned on me then that the Elves could not destroy the crystal. Who then? And then it came to me. It had to be ME!

Immediately I set out for the Black Stone Monastery. I traveled mostly by night and found shelter in which to hide myself during the day. Priests were everywhere and their informants were everyone.

Once in awhile I would find a kindly soul who would let me work for food and shelter. But mostly I traveled alone and foraged from the land what I could get. It took me a week before I found myself walking the same path the Priest had walked that fateful day he had seen my father shoot the puffer in the air. I was tempted to spend one last time in my childhood memories but my resolve was that of a man. "I am no longer a child. I no longer need to nurse my memories of what used to be. It is time to take my part in the plan of life, to make my mark and be who I am."

I knew the monastery better than any outsider did. I also knew how to get in. I waited until darkness fell and, silently as possible, I stole up the valley to the sewer pipe. My sleigh was gone but the pipe was still there. Silently, I crawled in.

I crawled up the pipe realizing it was a lot smaller than I remembered. The grate was still dislodged and I forced my way through. Finally, I reached the inner stream, found a torch and lit it with my trusty twirly. "Just like old times," I mused to myself.

I made my way to the peephole of the torture chamber. "No one on the rack today. Things must be slow for the torture team. Perhaps Dwarg is losing his touch."

At the next peephole, I peered carefully in upon the altar chamber. There, in the middle of the room, upon the altar, sat the black crystal. It was held in place by the same golden, three-fingered hand. I looked up at the old trap door. "Too easy," I said to myself. "There is something too convenient about all this," I mumbled to myself as I climbed up the crypt walls to the trapdoor. "I can't believe they would leave something this valuable unguarded. It's too important to them." Still, I slipped onto the ledge. All my senses were on full alert. I knew something was not right.

The only weapon I carried was my faithful wrist levitator. On feet of feathers I tiptoed along the ledge. There was no person present in the chamber. Determined as I was, I quickly slid down the wall drape and without a moment's hesitation, landed on the floor. Still sensing no resistance, I dashed to the altar.

I reached out and grabbed the crystal. It would not budge. It was sealed in its place. I yanked hard and then again, harder. I heard a click from the ceiling. As I looked up the entire ceiling was covered by a net that began to fall upon me. "The perfect trap!"

My instincts were quick. I raised the levitator and beamed it at one side of the net. It folded upward. I dashed toward that side of the room and scampered up one of the wall tapestries. The net fell harmlessly to the floor.

Priests flooded the room. They came from the trap door, the ledge upon which I once hid as a child, from the window and doors, which were filled with them. I grabbed one of the ropes from the net and swung down toward the doorway. Two priests swung the door shut while others flung themselves in my direction. Using the levitator, I caused them to pile on top of each other.

Distracted as I was with handling the priests, I did not notice Dwarg crawl up through the trap door. Suddenly I was lifted off my feet and flung against the wall. I hit with such force that, for a moment, I lost my senses.

"You are not the only one who knows how to use levitation. Ha! Ha! Ha!" he crowed.

Again, I was lifted. This time I rose quickly to the ceiling and then I was flung instantly toward the floor. I barely had time to cushion my fall. As I hit, I rolled with a dozen priests grasping for my body.

I beamed a quick thrust of levitation toward Dwarg but he ignored it, laughing. "You have never been trained on levitation as a weapon. Here, let me show you."

He lifted the net, priests and all, and swirled it around me. I thrust the levitator at one edge of the net and jumped through. "Very good!" he shouted, "for a beginner." Then, without me noticing it, he lifted a club that one of the priests had brought into the room. He shot the club directly at the back of my head. Something warned me and I ducked but, as I was scrambling to get away from the still swirling net, the club hit me in the shoulder. I went down under the force of the blow, feeling as though something had just broken my shoulder and crushed the breath out of me.

Instantly, the priests were all over me. Dwarg leapt down beside me staring me in the face. "I wanted to keep you alive so you can enter the Grid. Ha! Ha! Ha!" he roared. All I could think to say was, "Someday I will give you a toy."

"To the chamber with him!" he roared. Still wrapped in the net, they lifted me over their heads and, with Dwarg leading the way, took me to the torture room. Immediately, I was bound upon the rack. In spite of the best of my intentions, I was lost to the power of the black crystal.

Kris Kringle and the Black Crystal

Chapter Twelve

The Shifting of the Field

The Elves were busy. "Crystal, are you ready?" It was Comcom.

"Ready Captain!" She sat upon the sleigh, reins in her hands. The reindeer were ready to go and a bag of toys was in the back.

"Remember, in order to get him out of there, we must seed the Grid of Agony in such a way that each participant chooses, of their own free will, to change. It can't be done in any other way."

"I understand Captain." She sat determined, the lines of her fair features set hard against what was to come.

Then Doray took over. "Comcom and Misty will be with you. I won't tell you there is nothing to fear because we are being monitored by the Delovians. The hope we share is that they do not understand what we are doing and it will appear harmless. We've been over this before. Anything more?"

"No sir." She was as ready as anyone could ever be.

"OK. Let's get him out of there."

At a signal from Doray, the sleigh, drawn by the eight reindeer and with Comcom, Misty and Crystal securely inside, leapt forward. Almost immediately they disappeared into the space between time. Crystal shivered in the moment of cold and then instantly found herself and her little companions in a forest just outside a small cottage. As she landed the sleigh, she noticed a little boy playing by a small pond.

"Malevolent's father is less than three years of age. Perfect!" she said as she reached back into her bag of toys. She searched for and found the little boat. She gently lifted it from the bag and placed it next to her heart. She hugged it once more giving it a super charge of that special frequency of love. Then she unfolded herself from the sleigh and moved toward the little boy.

He looked up and fear filled his face. She stopped. "Hello," she said gently. "I came to play with my boat. Is it all right?" He looked at her and was about to run home, but she said, "Do you know how a boat works?" Without hesitation she continued, "Look. I will show you."

His curiosity held him in place as she waded into the shallow edge of the pond. She looked down into the deeper water and shuddered, realizing it was this very water that may have helped cause the death of so many people in the future. She let the boat float gently in the water. Guiding it with her fingertips, she pushed it in the direction of the little boy.

She laughed, loving children and loving their play, which helped him suddenly feel at ease. The tension melted away as he stepped forward. She stepped back and motioned with her hand. He approached the boat. It floated toward him. Tentatively, he reached out with his hand. His finger touched the boat. An amazing warmth flowed from the boat into his hand, up his arm and down through his entire body. He was as if frozen for a moment. Then he giggled. The warmth spread through his entire body, filling his heart and spilling down into the water, filling the pond.

She backed away. "Would you like to keep the boat?" He looked at her in an imploring look. "It's yours. I have another one. Have fun," she said as she backed toward the sleigh. She and the Elves sat in silence watching the little boy play with the boat. He waded in the water fearlessly, following the boat.

It drifted into deeper water and the boy followed. When he stepped into the deeper water, he suddenly sank from sight! Crystal jumped to her feet and was about to leap to his rescue, but Misty placed her hand on Crystal's arm cautioning her to wait. The boy's natural responses took over and he rose to the surface, sputtering and then began to paddle like a little dog. He paddled himself out and around the boat and pushed it back to shore.

"Whew! I am glad that's over," Crystal sighed as she sat back down.

"Let's get out of here. We can monitor this from another place," said Comcom.

Crystal picked up the reins and jingled the bells. The boy looked up just in time to see the little sleigh and the eight tiny reindeer leap into the air and disappear from sight. He raised his hand but there was no one there to see. He went back to playing with his boat. There was a wonderful contented smile upon his face.

"One more delivery." She could hear Doray's voice though the coldness of betweeness.

"We are ready," she heard Comcom reply, but it was more in her mind than in her ears that she could hear. In an instant they popped through into a place surrounded by open fields. A little country cottage was nestled under some towering pines.

"This could be a little tricky," she mumbled to herself as she reached back into the bag of toys. She located the book and drew it out. She thumbed briefly through the pages, with colored illustrations meticulously hand printed and on every page. "We don't even know if they can read," she exclaimed.

"The holoscan indicates that he could read later in his life, so let's step right up and let's do it," said Misty.

Feeling hesitant, Crystal stepped out of the sleigh. She knew the young couple was expecting a baby and that they would have no means by which to support the child. In desperation, he would steal from the wine maker. In the process he would become a drunkard, be caught, disgraced and banished. He would, according to the holoscan, seek employment in the city but there he would be shanghaied.

His wife and son would never again see him or know what happened. In desperation, she would leave the child on a farmer's doorstep. During the night, the child was attacked by a farm dog. The farmer would rescue the child but the scars would always show. Benton would never be considered normal. A large child, he would grow to become a giant who abused those who taunted him. Isolated, he was treated as the monster he would become.

"It's the only way to get the father to realize what happens," whispered Misty. "That book is the story of his life if he takes to drinking and steals the wine."

"Well, it's a chance," mumbled Crystal. "But it seems like a long one," she said as she turned away. She walked slowly toward the house. Instinctively, she paused to pick a few flowers on the way. When she got to the door, she knocked quietly.

A young woman, heavy with child, opened the door a crack. "What do you want?" she asked with heavy suspicion. For a moment, Crystal felt like backing out. But only for a moment did she hesitate.

"I am sorry to bother you but I heard you were expecting and so I came to visit." She smiled her most winning smile and the door opened a little more. "Who are you?" asked the woman, her eyes squinting as if to see more clearly.

"My name is Crystal and I live down the way." She smiled again and the door opened a little more. "I brought you a little gift because I know what you must be going through. Please, can we be friends?" The door opened a little more and the woman's eyes softened. "You want to be friends?"

"If you like…" the words hung in the air. They looked at each other and for just a moment a twinkle passed between them. "It would be fine to have a friend," the woman said with a growing smile. She held the door open, an invitation for Crystal to enter.

The one-room home was clean but impoverished. Only the bare necessities were evident. Handmade furniture, a bare plank table and a bed of straw with one blanket in the corner left the impression of barest survival. Crystal seemed not to notice and found an old jar for the flowers. "Any water?" she asked. "Oh yes," the woman replied. "I have to go to the well but there's a little here. Let's use it. I love flowers but I haven't taken the time lately. I have been pretty weak with the baby coming on."

"It will be a boy." Crystal almost swore to herself. "Damn. I shouldn't have said that," she thought to herself. "Really?" The woman was suddenly a little cautious. "How would you know that?" She looked at Crystal from the side of her eyes. Crystal's caution flags went up. This was an age of witch hunts and she didn't want to cause trouble. Having handled special children, she knew the magic of a twinkle and looked deeply into the woman's eyes and twinkled back, "I have a wonderful gift for you."

The young mother-to-be relaxed again. "I hope it is a boy." Then she looked up, "A gift for me?" "Yes," giggled Crystal excitedly. "It's a book with lots of pictures." She took the book from beneath her cloak and gave it an excited hug as she handed the book to the woman.

At the touch of the book, warmth flooded through her. It seemed to reach into every pore of her body. "Why," she exclaimed, "it is almost as though the book brings me comfort! I have never seen a book before. Only the priests have such things. It is a treasure beyond price." As she held the book to her breast, she smiled and closed her eyes. "I have never felt such comfort."

"May I read it to you?" asked Crystal in almost a whisper. "Can you read?" asked the woman. Realizing it was a stupid question, she continued, "Oh would you? And then I can tell it to my husband."

Carefully and lovingly, Crystal led the woman through the story. "I am afraid it is a sad story," she began.

But the woman did not mind. "Much of my life has been sad," she explained.

So picture by picture, Crystal told the story and explained the carefully written words. Finally, after the child becomes a priest and tortures people in the Black Stone Monastery, the woman is crying. "It is a horrible story," she wept. "How could this happen to anyone?"

Crystal looked deeply into the woman's eyes. "You must tell this story to your husband." The woman was taken back. "But he is a humble wine taster. He would not ..." her voice trailed off. Realization struck her. Crystal placed the book carefully in her hands.

"Please. Just read the story to him and trust. All will be well." She rose to her feet and hugged the dazed woman. "Promise?" she asked, looking deeply into the woman's eyes.

"I promise. Of course! I promise! I promise. Will you come again?" The woman wanted some sort of support, maybe even wanted her to stay at least until her husband came home.

"We will see," Crystal said with a smile as she stepped out and closed the door behind her. She ran to the sleigh. "Go!" They whisked out of sight. "Whew. That was tough." She felt the shiver of between times and popped back into the cave where the ASTAR team awaited their return.

"Just in time!" shouted Doray. "Look." As she stepped into the Starship Doray was excitedly pointing at the holoscan. Benton was undoing my wrist irons. I was barely conscious. "You have suffered enough for one lifetime," he said, taking me up in his arms and carrying me out of the torture chamber.

As we passed the door of the altar room, the voice of Dwarg boomed through the door, "Bring him here, Benton."

"Ohhhh. Can't I just go and get him?" whispered Crystal. "He looks so, sooo ... spent up."

"Shhhh. Just watch," whispered Doray. "Every problem has its own solution and this solution is deeper than anyone has ever dreamed."

Benton, so obedient for so many years, automatically carried me into the room where Dwarg sat upon the altar. The black crystal was in his hands. "So you think he has suffered enough for one lifetime, do you? You have not begun to comprehend the suffering he is yet to endure. You think you can decide?"

"I know only that this man is good ..." but he never got to finish his sentence.

"You miserable lout! I'll tell you what you know and what you don't know!"

A great bolt of black lightening leapt from the crystal. It caught Benton and I full in its power and lifted us above the floor. It twirled us around and froze Benton and I together. Pain shot through us and rattled us to the bone. We were being burned and disintegrated, cell by cell. It was like my own brain was frying on a frying pan.

Suddenly, Delpha appeared in front of Dwarg. "Dwarg, what are you doing?" she asked coyly and shrieked "Ha! Ha! Ha!"

"Hello, my dear. I am tending to the Sender as you can see. I am so glad you can watch. I thought this meddling cockroach sealed the crack in the cosmos. He placed that secret device in the black hole. How then, is it you are able to communicate with me so clearly my sweet?"

"Oh, you darling. I am outside our anti-matter continuum and I am sure you will be glad to hear that I am almost upon your sector with my armada. I wanted to let you know so you could prepare for my little gift." Again she shrieked in laughter.

"Little gift? What have you cooked up now, my dearest? Something up to your usual cuisine I hope?" He grinned an evil grin.

"Oh yes. It will warm even your heart. My, it looks like you are having fun. Are you ready to do that to the entire space-time continuum of matter?" She twirled as she spoke.

Dwarg looked up. She had his full attention. Benton and I were unceremoniously dumped on the floor. "You think we could do this to the entire continuum? All matter? Oh, my darling, you are so evil. So delightfully evil!"

"I have a new seed — a very special seed, my love — one that takes matter and uses it to create a new black hole. Ha, Ha, Ha! Anything it touches in the continuum is transformed into anti-matter!"

"But what about the energy? You have found a way to capture the extra energy and use it to create the new black hole?" His eyes were wide with anticipation.

"Oh, you are quick, my dearest. Prepare for the best party of our lives and there is nothing they can do about it. Finish that roach off and get ready to join the party!" She twirled closer to him.

"What party?" he almost gasped. "What are you planning, my darling?"

"You shall see. You shall see such a sight as never has been seen." Then, coming to a stop near him, she leaned in close to his ear and whispered, "I have the bomb of bombs, the maker of black holes. I am setting it to go off over Bethlehem at the moment of his birth!" she cackled in wicked glee.

"The end of the Master Sender!?" He was visibly taken back. "But …"

"Ha! Ha! Ha!" she screeched.

"Even the great Dwarg is speechless! Ha, Ha, Ha. You amaze me, my precious. We are on our way there now. Get rid of that one there. I shall get rid of the Master one and then we will finish this job!" Dwarg's face was thoughtful for a moment and then he brightened. It was as though he grasped the immensity of her plan.

"You are going to plant the black hole bomb to explode over Bethlehem on the night of the birth of the Master Sender, ending his power forever! It is ingenious. He and his entire dominion, all the worlds and galaxies, will collapse into the new black hole. They will be transformed into pure black matter. The energy from all that matter! For Delovians use! As we will it to be done!"

He paused for a moment and then bowed to her. "A more ambitious plan than even I could have conceived." As he raised his head, "I am on my way …huh?" He never got to finish his statement. Malevolent had entered the room. He stood on the opposite side of Dwarg from Benton and I and held his hands outstretched.

I found myself surrendering, letting go and trusting to a deeper force, one I only sensed was present deep within me. I remembered. I remembered my father, his love and his trust in me. I remembered the visitation I had while I was still on the rack. I remembered the being whose love was total, universal — the Master Sender. I made room for him in my heart of hearts.

I remembered our many lives together and of our great love for one another. I remembered our love for children everywhere. I remembered the toys, hugging them and feeling the frequency of his love. I remembered the woman who attempted to come to me when I was with my father and the Master Sender. I could see her face clearly. It was Crystal! The realization raised me above the pain and the powers of the Grid of Agony.

I raised my hand toward Dwarg. "His love I send to you." A bolt of white light pierced the darkness of the Grid of Agony. The dark crystal exploded in Dwarg's hands.

"Nooo!" Delpha screamed as the white light surrounded Dwarg and jumped into the holoscan surrounding her as well.

"It works both ways," I heard a voice say. I looked toward the voice. He, the Master Sender, stood across the room from me. Malevolent, Benton and I formed a triangle around Dwarg and the holoscan of Delpha. He stood at its apex.

"Noooooooo ... !" Dwarg seemed to disappear into the stream of white light that emanated from Malevolent, Benton and I and the Master Sender. The light literally sucked Dwarg into the holoscan. It swarmed around Delpha and then they disappeared from the room. Benton and I collapsed.

I awoke in the arms of the Master Sender. "Well done, Nicholas. Well done."

Suddenly, Crystal and my Elfin friends swept into the room. She held the reins of the sleigh that was still pulled by eight tiny reindeer. "We must go now," was all she said. It was all she needed to say. I could hear the footsteps of the priests running down the hall.

I looked at Benton, then at Malevolent. He looked deeply into my eyes. "We are needed here. Come and visit. The children here, of all ages, will need your services."

"I will return on Christmas Eve," I said with a chuckle.

He looked perplexed. "Oh, on the birth of the Master Sender." He roared with a laughter that filled the room and flooded the halls of the monastery. He waved his hand in acknowledgment as we swept out of the room. Later, much later, I learned about a new star that was born the evening of the birth of the Master Sender. I sat next to Crystal in the sleigh. The warmth of her, our legs and arms touching began to flow through me. I was healing. I was getting stronger by the second and her presence next to me captured more than my interest in healing.

The Shifting of the Field

Chapter Thirteen

The Elfin Project

"**L**ove is a living thing!" exclaimed Misty. "Look at it grow."

"Yes," mused Comcom. "It is changing the Grid."

"That's not what I meant," said Misty, smirking. The Elves were amused and pleased that Crystal and I have found each other. Without interfering, we both knew they were watching or sensing every move we made.

"But we need more Senders," said Doray. "To really seed the grid with love we must have Senders from around the planet. Look at this." He pointed into the holoscan at the Grid of Agony. "Look how a lack of education feeds into the grid. Look how their personal and collective greed, pride and abuse habits, are still causing the grid to grow! It is still creeping outward!"

We watched as the holoscan spanned a projection of the years ahead. The grid could be seen as slowly growing. I stood next to Crystal, our arms touching and feeling the flow of energy between us. In spite of the grid, I felt happy.

"You would think humans could learn to hug their toys," murmured Solah. And, almost to herself Misty reflected, "It's not just a matter of *giving* toys. They must be *infused with love*. Most humans have this ability but it seems to be buried in their subconscious. Some even pray for others but they must learn to *intensify their love* feelings, get them aligned with their own potential Sender and put that love into action in their physical surroundings."

"*Love is alive*. All we have to do is give it a chance," exclaimed Mefa, more than a little frustrated with humanity. "I just wish more people would choose love."

"I like that. **Choose love**. Makes a good slogan," Comcom suggested. Suddenly the holoscan popped up with all kinds of billboards with "Choose Love!" slogans. Everyone laughed.

"Well," said Misty, "toys are ideal for transmitting love. They have no other purpose and they can store great amounts of love. They can even give it out in little bits, one moment at a time. Furthermore, the more the toys are used, the more love is manifested."

"Yeah, and the more of a chance there is that people will choose to give love to others," quipped Doray. "They can even choose to give love back to the toys. The more love they choose, the more love they have to give people."

"The more a child loves a toy, the more love goes back into the field," said Mefa. She was working on plans for a toyshop. Her fingers played inside the holoscan and her mind was busy thinking things through. "Toys can be infused with love," she mused. "When a love toy comes in contact with the Grid of Agony, the love transforms the Grid. Love changes agony when it's effective love."

"Sounds like we need more love toys," Comcom summarized.

"Any toy, any gift, infused with love, is a seed," said Crystal. "It grows when it is planted and nurtured."

"So, because a love toy has its own vibration, it can strengthen the Field of Love. Hummm. I wonder if just anyone can send love." Comcom joined Mefa in the holoscan.

"Well the Master Sender's love sure did the job on the black hole but most humans don't recognize a Sender. That's why there is so much agony on this planet," said Doray.

"Unless they are touched by love — then they recognize the Sender," argued Mefa. "Look at their microtubules. Every human has direct access. They have openings in the quantum foam. Each opening is portal directly connected to their own unique fullest potential self."

She shifted the holoscan screen so Crystal could see the microtubules and watch what was happening inside them. Images and a field appeared inside the tubulin wall.

"That means that every human is a Sender?" I asked. "Yes but they are all in embryo," Crystal suggested. "Once they connect, kaboom!"

"Kaboom?" Misty raised an eyebrow. It did not slow Crystal down. "Perhaps parents could learn to give love toys to their children. They could hug their toys — infuse them with their own personal love, and Kaboom!" she said.

"And parents who treat their children badly?" Mefa asked. "Like those who even abuse their children? Could their love affect the Grid?" There was a moment of silence as everyone thought about it. Then Misty whispered, "If it comes from their Sender it can't do anything but add to the Field of Love."

And Solah said, "The Field of Love can create a quantum leap in the consciousness of humankind."

"It would take a lot of toys," Comcom said as he shook his head.

And, before anyone could even take a breath, "We can make them!" Crystal cried. "With some help from the Elfin society, it could be done!"

There are moments when, in the history of life, a certain magic is taking place. It is a time of peril and a time of peace. It is a time of chaos and a time of new order. It is a time when the universe seems to come together. Where once was doubt, now comes trust. Where once was darkness, now comes light. In a world of confusion, everything suddenly makes sense. "It will have to be done in a place where the powers of darkness and the priests of the Black Stone Monastery cannot interfere," declared Comcom.

The group fell silent. Would it be possible to create enough Love Toys to make a difference in the Grid of Agony? Where in the world could a safe place ever be found? How could it be organized?

It was Crystal who brought the gathering into order. "ASTAR!" she declared. "Let's ask ASTAR. The holoscan can help us find a place!" And so it was that we began to search for a safe place, one away from the powers of darkness that could be used to make toys for the children of Earth.

As the holoscan showed various castles, remote cottages, deep forest valleys and other hidden places where the Elves would be able to live, Crystal and I were realizing we wanted more and more to be alone together. Signaling her with my eyes and a slight nod of my head (I am sure that all the Elves were completely aware), we left the starship and walked along the path into the forest. It was wonderful to be with her. As we walked, we talked about many things, the forest, the hidden forest under the soil, how life reproduces itself and how information is continually exchanged.

"Crystal, why did Benton free me from the rack? And what caused the amazing change in Malevolent so they both actually turned on Dwarg?"

She beamed in her quiet coy way and said, "Dwarg was able to use both Benton and Malevolent as part of the Grid of Agony because of the abuse they had both suffered as children. Both were abandoned by their parents and both suffered abuse."

I broke in. "So both became susceptible to the forces of entropy?"

"Yes," she said. I found myself somehow drawn to look at her lips. They drew me closer but she continued as she ducked under my arm and continued to walk. "In Benton's case, his father was a wine-taster and they were very poor. In desperation, to provide for his family, he stole wine from the winery. He began to drink and was caught. The authorities were going to put him in prison but the wine owner agreed to a lesser punishment of public shame and banishment. Disgraced and unable to get work, he left the country and sought work in the city."

"Oh, that's good. Did he find a job?" I was now gently backing her toward the broad trunk of a huge tree.

"Actually," she said, "no one ever heard from him again."

"What?" I was almost distracted. "That's really sad. I would think his being gone put her in a pretty desperate place." I had my arm around Crystal but she was still teasing me.

"In fact, she was starving. She could see that if she did not do something her baby would die. Rather than just give up, she prepared the child as best she could, wrapped him in her only blanket and slipped into the wine owner's yard late one evening. It was a desperate step to save the live of her baby son. She shook her head seeming to realize how desperate the woman must have been. She laid him on the step of the house, knocked on the door and ran. Before anyone came to answer the door, a wild dog discovered the baby. It attempted to drag the baby away and, in doing so, bit into his face."

"The baby was Benton?" I asked. "Yes," she replied. "He lived but he has had a terrible scar. The wine owner's wife was a kindly soul and took the baby in but, because he was so ugly, she arranged to give him to the Monastery. Benton was raised to be a priest but he was always an outsider."

"He was big and he was ugly. It must have been very difficult for him," I suggested. "He was never accepted by his peers. He worked the sweatshops until he became Malevolent's right-hand man." She was ducking behind a giant fern and I was trying to catch her, all the while being drawn by the magic of her moving body.

"Ah yes, Malevolent," I said, just as I caught the back of her tunic and began to draw her back toward me. "His story was even more tragic," she proclaimed as she jumped high into the air and back somersaulted over my head. I spun around but she was already out of reach.

"Born to a proud and headstrong father, Malevolent was always ...assertive!" I dove for her foot but she spun away as she almost spat the word toward me as she skipped toward a large toadstool. "In order to control him, his father used to punish him by sticking his head ..." She could not continue. "It was just so terrible Nicholas."

I stopped chasing her and walked up and put my arm around her. She looked up at me and then just leaned against my chest. For a moment I was spellbound. I forgot Benton, Malevolent, the Black Stone Monastery and the Grid of Agony. I felt inner warmth pulsing through my body. A deep peace flooded through me. It was something I had never felt before, like a rising tide of that lifted me and suspended me in its essence. I just wanted her there, always in my arms.

She pulled a little away as she dried her eyes. "His father almost drowned before he was 3 years old. It was why he such a fixation on water."

I must have looked confused because she continued to tell the story. "It began, as far as ASTAR could find, one fateful day, before Malevolent's father was three years old. He was playing in the shallow end of a pond not far from his home. His father, that would be Malevolent's grandfather — decided to teach him a lesson on 'being a man.' It was a macho thing, I guess."

She gave me a quick peck on my left cheek. "He picked him up and threw him in — into the deep end!"

"You mean he just threw him in?" I was quite astonished.

"Yes. The poor child was so frightened, he gulped water and almost drowned. His father dragged him out but it was in total disgust. From that point on, he treated the boy as though he were worthless. Malevolent's father grew up hating water."

"And everything else." I sat down on the trunk of a large fallen tree. I motioned for her to sit with me.

"He was angry at all men and abusive to everyone," she sighed as she snuggled down next to me.

"So he abused his own son?" I questioned as I reached up and gently moved a lock of hair that hung over her left eye.

"He used water to punish Malevolent. He was not much of a father…" she bent forward and lightly kissed the tip of my nose.

"Maybe that's why he sought the Church," I suggested.

"He sought an ultimate father and I guess God was the only one around," she ventured.

"He sought to 'do his father's will' and became a priest!" I was amazed at her insight.

"That's why we needed the hairs," she commented.

"Hairs? What hairs?" I turned to look her full in the face. She was so beautiful I almost lost my trend of thought again.

"Well," she replied, "the Elves' researched with ASTAR to find what might make a real impact on the grid. They needed an opening within the 'quantum wave of potentiality,' as they say. They realized that human history might really be changed and they could enter into that part of time they called 'the critical point' in the past, that time when decisions were made that drew people into the Grid of Agony."

I still looked perplexed and she saw it and she countered, "We can shift the field!" she exclaimed. "The field?" I shot back. She looked at me like I was asleep. I guess I was because I was watching her lips instead of listening to her words. She looked at me and laughed. "Nicholas, Nicholas." She kissed me fully and melted into my arms. "That's how the Elfin project got started in the first place," she purred between continued kisses.

I let go of her. "The Elfin project? What is the Elfin project?" I was beginning to focus again. She sighed. "It's the project the Elves have been helping with."

I shook my head in frustration. "What are you talking about?"

"I know," she paused. I was about to ask her again but she held up her hand and placed a finger on my lips. It stopped me. "I know" she repeated. "I will tell you all about the toy-making operation, the seeding of the quantum field, the …"

"Seeding the quantum field?" I interrupted.

"Yes. Oh, well," she sighed, "Now is a good a time as any. I guess we will never be together as long as that mind of yours is not satisfied."

"But …" I was about to explain when she interrupted.

"No buts." She took my hand and pulled me back toward the cave. "Come on," she teased. "I will show you."

Then, like a young deer, she suddenly was jumping up ahead and laughing, then running around a tree and pretending to hide. Even though I was in a daze, mostly over her, I knew that the Field of Love was more powerful than anything. It was the field of life. I have learned from ASTAR that every life form is cooperative, negotiating and in symbiosis with every other life form. I noticed that, even in my playful pursuit of her, our direction always led us closer to the starship.

As we entered the cave she bounded ahead and into the starship. I was close behind her and heard as she bolted out to Comcom, "Can we use ASTAR for a moment?" Doray moved back and Crystal turned to look into the holoscan. "Stick your head in here," she motioned. Inside I could see her head and then she said, "Focus first on the research of the Elves."

I could see the Elves as ASTAR scanned into the hair samples of Malevolent and Benton. I watched as they discovered the microtubules, found the holodynes that make up each person's memories and made note of their areas of non-organization. "What are those areas?" I asked.

"Those are the fields of quantum potential. They haven't been organized yet," she said matter-of-factly that I was still confused. She must have sensed it because she said, "Those areas give us choice." She waited a moment and then added, "If everything was already organized, there would be no choice. So these fields are capable of being organized by us, by our choices. We can choose agony or love, for example."

"These are in every cell of our bodies?" I asked even though I could see it clearly on the holoscan. "They fill each microtubule and every living thing has microtubules. It's where advanced consciousness begins to emerge."

I didn't even pretend to understand all that, but I knew she knew and I knew I was getting to know her a lot better. I wanted to know more and more about her. If she was interested in microtubules or how hair is analyzed, then so was I.

"Once the Elves discovered the reasons for the abusive natures of Malevolent and Benton, we figured out how to seed their past with toys of Love," she said.

"You mean the Elfin project is about seeding the past with love?" It hit me then, right in the face. "Exactly!" she beamed. "And it's more."

Suddenly, I was all ears. "That means..." I never got to finish the sentence.

"That the Grid of Agony can be transformed by..." she never got to finish her sentence.

"The Field of Love!" I almost shouted.

We popped out of the holoscan at the same moment. I hugged her, took her by the hands and we danced, hopping up and down in a circle in the little space of the starship. "Look," she said as she let go of my hands and almost pushed my head back into the holoscan. "See how it transformed the entire family life patterns of both Malevolent and Benton!" I watched as their lives unfolded in front of me.

"Why both families became different!" I watched in amazement as the history of the past rewrote itself. "If it will work for them, it will work for anyone!" She said with a confident air of triumph. I was proud of her. Then I got the message: "We can change the past." "Yes," she said with such an air of confidence I wanted to start kissing her all over again.

"So that's why my father's workshop was still there and all my toys. They never were destroyed. We relived that part of history. Amaaaazing!" I was beginning to sense that deeper part of myself that had always guided me.

"That's partly it," she said.

"Partly?" I almost stammered. "What do you mean partly? There's more?"

"Yes." Leaning over next to my ear she whispered, "We can bring the future into the now."

At that point I wondered if I would ever catch up to her. Then I began to realize, "So my father's workshop — all the toys he made, the very spirit of his work — is still alive." I felt like a kid again. All his tools, the magic of the mystery of the memories, were so potent that I had to go visit. I pulled my head out of the holoscan. "It's true!"

"And even better!" she teased. I waited, my mouth open. She put a finger under my chin and pushed up so my mouth closed. "The Elfin project has brought the future into the project. The project is so successful I must show you..." but she never finished her sentence.

"I must go!" And I was gone. I flew from the cave on feet as fleet as ever I knew. My home and my father's workshop were all renewed, restored to its former state! The Elves —

they did it! Somehow they were able to restructure my father's toyshop! Over the crest and through the forest I ran. Not as I had once run, as a child who was devastated and lost, but as a man — a renewed man who knew himself and had grasped his destiny. Now I could come to peace with the greatest loss of my life. There was hope! There was a way to seed the Grid of Agony with the Field of Love. That is the message of my father's entire life. Love Toys!

I came upon the meadow and there, in the middle, still tucked under the huge pine tree, was the shop. I could see where the silver wire was still threaded high into the top of the tree. My heart raced at the thought of the toys. Were they still there? I slowed to a walk as I took it all in. Was this a dream or was the other a dream? And father? What of my father? I wondered where he was. "Father?" I said rather weakly. I was hoping against hope that he would still be here as well. But the shop was empty.

The sunlight seeped through the same old cracks between the wooden planks and flooded the floor through the old window on one side of the shop above the desk. Speckles of dust lingered in the air, floating like little worlds through the galaxy of my father's creations. His tools were there as were the papers, toys and works of art I had learned to love. It was only a small part of the true measure of the man.

I picked up the dancing children music box, twisted the key and watched as each little carved figure pivoted as if in perfect harmony with the musical melody that wafted from the little chimes within. I knew exactly how he had made those chimes, carved those little human dancers and put it all together. It tugged at my heart that I could not tell him of my appreciation for all he had taught me.

"Nicholas?"

I spun around. He stood in the doorway, the sunlight at his back. I was about to rush to embrace him but I could see through him and knew then, he was truly no longer of this world. "Father," I cried, "Oh father. I..." My words could not come. I knew not what to say. I stumbled toward him my love flowing over into my consciousness in such tides that I felt overwhelmed with joy and I almost fainted. He held up his hand, motioning me to stop.

It was then I noticed the other Sender. He stood beside my father. I stopped in amazement. "Yes Nicholas. It is a greater workshop in which I work now."

"But Father, the Grid of Agony, the suffering of the children, it is not over. The Elves say that the Grid is growing and that humans have to learn to love, to seed the grid with..."

"I know, my son. Everything is known and from the beginning of time we choose it to be so." Every word he said reached deep down into the reservoir of my being. "You are vital to the game."

"You mean all this, the pain, the suffering, the grid...?" I felt suspended in time. "Yes, my son. Each player chooses his part. Even you."

My mind was trying to catch up. "I do not understand," I murmured. My knees were getting weak, I wanted to sit down. "How could I have chosen to...?"

As if reading my mind, the Master Sender said, "Step out of time, Nicholas. Sense the real essence of yourself."

I looked inward and an infinite peace filled my being. There, walking toward me was another radiant being. He was tall, powerful and clear in mind and heart. His joy of living overflowed to everyone around him. I stepped forward to greet him and discovered it was ME! It was ME at my fullest potential, my Full Potential Self!

He embraced me in a way so wonderful that there are no words to describe our meeting. He entered my body, filled my mind and heart and flooded me with a confidence I had never known. I looked through his eyes and sensed his knowledge and intelligence. I looked at my father and the Master Sender and took my place beside them.

"Yes," said my father. "Now you know there are levels within levels in which the games of life are played. You know that Malevolent and Benton and all of the others who set their foot upon this planet came to play their part so they can discover who they are at the deepest level of reality. It is in this remembering that they once again can assert their true nature. We are beings of love, born to transform the Grid of Agony."

"But life on earth, it could end!" I moaned. Then I caught myself. I knew my words were spoken by a younger version of myself. They did not come from my Full Potential Self. I heard my father say, "Human life truly could end as we know it now, unless people discover their true natures. All people have the intelligence, love and power to make a difference in the Grid of Agony. They must remember who they are and choose to act accordingly."

"The Grid of Agony?" I asked it as a question.

My father picked right up on the subject. "It, too, could take over. The black hole waits, ready to consume this entire planet, even our entire galaxy, if we so choose." My father actually smiled as he said this.

"You are needed here, Father. Please, come and be with me." Even as I said the words I knew my inner child was trying to get some reassurance.

"You have everything you need. The Elves will help. The Galactic Council has agreed to grant you special powers in order to overcome the Delovian effects of the Grid of Agony."

His statement drew me out of my inner pleadings. "Special powers? What does that mean?" I was anxious and I could not yet resist asking questions.

"It means, my son, that you will be able to travel in time. You will be able to take toys, infuse them with love, and seed them into the Grid of Agony until all its effects have been neutralized. You are to become truly a Santa if you so choose."

"I will do everything I can, Father. But the children are enslaved in the sweatshops and the authorities do not allow toys. Parents do not trust anyone..." I could have gone on and on. He cut me short.

"Precisely, my son. This is why you are needed." He said it with that familiar twinkle in his eye. "Ho! Ho! Ho!" he laughed with a full bellied laugh. He was his old self again and more, much more, than I could have imagined. My heart leapt to his laughter. "Enjoy your journey, my son. We shall always be with you!" Raising his hand in farewell, he and the Master Sender were gone in the twinkle of an eye.

I sat alone in my father's workshop, remembering the good times we use to share when I was a child. I remembered everything that had happened since that first sleigh ride. I realized now, that it had all started long before I was born, when, outside of time and space, I first made my choice to come to earth — to take a vacation! Life was a vacation from love! A vacation from intelligence! I came here to lose myself from my real Self so I could rediscover myself!

There, among the memories of my childhood, I realized I came here to Earth to enter the games of life, to deal with the Grid of Agony, to assert my true nature and seed it with the Field of Love. I now had a new alignment with my Full Potential Self and an admonition to "Enjoy the journey" from my father.

My mind took me through the multitudes involved in the game of life and the varieties of the games being played, and I began to see my special place in what will happen in the future. To be able to enter a game at any time, at any point and seed it with love toys — what an opportunity! "Thank you Delovians, for helping create my part in this great game." Without the opposition, no game would be possible. Life would be boring. "And thank you, priests of the Black Stone Monastery! You play your parts so well!"

I stood and looked around for tools with which to make toys. As was usual for me, my mind began to work on the practical problems that now faced me in my new mission. I worried having the shop so close to the monastery. I wondered how it could be done if I had to work alone, how I could even begin to supply the number of toys that would be needed. Perhaps a few well-placed toys would be enough to turn the tide on the growing agony that faced the people.

I thought of Crystal, her part in the plan and how she tried to leave the group in the Place of Planning and come to me. But she was held back by the Master Sender. Perhaps my own choice could make the plan more interesting. I was suddenly gripped by an idea and I knew what to do.

Gathering some wood, I lit the forge. As the flames grew higher, I took a small rock heavy laden with silver. I pounded it clear of most of the granite and placed it into the crucible. With a pair of my father's tongs, I placed the crucible carefully over the flame and left it there.

While I was waiting for it to turn into liquid silver, I lifted a small ball of molding wax. Taking some of my father's carving tools, I began to carve the wax into a perfect ring. Then, around one side of the ring, I carved eight tiny reindeer pulling a sleigh.

It felt good to use my creative energies as I took the plaster casting clay and encased the wax ring in plaster, leaving two holes. I could pour the molten silver into the hole on the top and I knew that the hole in the bottom would allow the wax to run through when it got hot. When it was ready, the silver was a steaming hot liquid. Carefully I poured it into the hole at the top of the cast. It bubbled a little but finally ran smoothly through until only pure silver came out the bottom hole. I let it sit and cool. Then I began to chip away the cast as I had seen my father do so many times. Out came a beautiful silver ring.

I touched up the carvings so they were perfect and then, taking a special tool, I carved three special words on the inside of the ring. Wrapping the ring in a special velvet cloth, I stuffed it in my pocket. Then I gathered up every tool and toy I could carry and began the journey back to the cave.

Halfway there, I met Crystal. She had been waiting for me from a discrete distance but now she could wait no more. When she saw me coming, she ran toward me and, in spite of my heavy load, jumped up on me, wrapping both her legs around my waist and giving me a big kiss as we both fell over backwards. "Oh, Nicholas! I have missed being with you. Is everything all right?"

"Everything is more than all right. I have just had a wonderful experience and I know now what we must do." I wanted to share my experience with her but she was too anxious to tell me something and she just blurted it out.

"I wanted to give you as much time as you needed but now we are late and we must hurry." She helped pull me to my feet.

"Why? What is happening?" I asked as she began picking up part of my load.

She blurted out, "We must go. I will tell you on the way. Hurry!" She began to walk, partly running up the path toward the cave. "Hurry! Please, we will be late for the meeting!"

I ran to catch up with her and, as I began to fall into pace with her, she said, "We have a grid alert!" My heart skipped a beat. "Is it bad?" I almost didn't want to ask.

We were just entering the cave so she said, "Come on. I'll show you on the holoscan."

We dropped the tools and toys at the door to the starship and Crystal leapt up the stairs and dashed to the holoscan. "ASTAR, show Nicholas the alert!"

Immediately I stuck my head into the holoscan and there, marching before me in the scanner, I could see thousands and thousands of men. Men in uniforms, countless men, holding strange weapons that shot fire and made loud noises. They rode in great chariots that had no horses and they could fly through the air as in great roaring birds. They rained terror and destruction down upon millions of people around the world.

Crystal was crying. "Oh, Nicholas!" she wept. "The grid will win. This is the future. We must do something!"

As I looked through the holoscan I saw so many people, so many acts of violence and so much agony that I could not stand to look. What I had seen so far on the holoscan was nothing compared to what was to come. I turned to my friends. "What is possible?" I asked.

"Anything is possible," said Comcom.

"Is it possible to transform the grid before it reaches this kind of strength?" I asked. "Can toys really make any difference at all?" The horror of what I had seen almost took hold on me. Standing directly in front of me and looking deeply into my eyes, Comcom said, "Humans have the ability to use their resources for toys of love or toys of war. The choice is within every human."

Everyone was silent for awhile, deep in thought. "Well I choose!" I suddenly said. "I choose toys of love but, from the looks of things, we are going to need a lot of toys."

Even Crystal smiled. Then she quietly commented, "I think we already have started." She had a gleam in her eye, one I had not seen before. It was filled with determination that matched my own.

She stood up. "We are already on the move."

"Started? On the move? What do you mean?" I began to wonder if I was the last person to know what was going on. As Doray heaved my sack of tools into the starship, we were all lifted slightly from our position and moved out of the cave. In a flash we were above the mountains and heading out across the steps of Russia into the northland, the vast white waste-land over which no man and few beasts can traverse; over a land so cold, so eternally frozen that just to look upon its face made my blood run cold. "Where on earth are we going?" I asked.

"To the Elfin project," she replied as she cuddled up against my arm. "Will someone please tell me what is going on? What exactly is the 'Elfin' project?" I was getting agitated at always having to catch up.

"Patience, my love," she cooed and I forgot what I was frustrated about. Before I could even get my bearings, the starship slowed and below I watched a giant iceberg open as if it were a blossoming flower. Into the center we dropped and my eyes widened with disbelief as the most amazing sight of my life greeted my eyes.

Under the ice grew an ancient forest of giant redwood and pine trees. As we stepped out of the Starship, the air was cool and fresh. Giant ferns, flowers, and plants of every kind flourished in deep black soil. Pathways, soft and clear, ran in every direction and the noise of life was everywhere. Birds and insects, animals of all kinds, lived here, under the ice! It was an inner world all its own, isolated completely from the outside world. No priests or armies could reach us here. As I stepped onto the path I felt an overwhelming sensation of coming home. As I looked around and listened, I could hear a steady beating in the background. It sounded like a factory in full production.

"What place is this?" I asked.

She turned, looking straight in my eyes. "While you were 'away' playing your 'suffering' games," she teased, "we were quite busy. Come, let me show you." Still teasing, she led me through the woods. Such beauty surrounded us that I wanted to stay and explore but she insisted, "Time is wasting and we have work to do."

"Work?" I wanted to resist but her ways were winning. I found myself unable to do anything but submit to her will. I followed as if I was a little sheep being led by its shepherd. Around a bend we began to emerge from the forest. A large and most wondrous building came into view. It was every color and shape one could imagine with little roof tops winding around towers of bigger ones, little windows within larger ones, and everything going together in a bazaar kind of coherence. Everywhere was life. And everywhere were Elves.

"Where did they all come from? How did this place get here?" I was having a hard time catching up.

"While you were..." she paused, "away, we were busy."

"Hello, Ms. Crystal," a businesslike Elf said as he bowed slightly toward her. "The West Wing is producing at full capacity now. We need your permission to advance the Left Wing another 45 percent in size. It will increase production by 150 percent approximately. Would that be OK?" He waited for her reply.

She thought for a moment and then added, "If we increase it another 10 percent and include a processing draft line, we might be able to milk it up to about a 65 percent increase." He looked a little confused so she added, "When we combine it with the robot line coming in from the Central platform." "Oh," he said. "Yes, of course. I will let Central know. Thank you, Chief," and off he ran.

"Central? Production? Robot line? *Chief?* What is going on?" I was still not catching on.

"This, my darling, is a toy factory. We produce toys." I must have frozen with my mouth open because she flicked her finger in and out of it so fast it brought me back to my senses. A toy factory!? I was dumbfounded. She smiled back at me. There was more to this woman that I realized. As it was still dawning on me, she took me by the hand and led me through a door.

We entered what she called "the factory" and what I saw was both the most wonderful and also the most overwhelming sight I could have ever imagined. Toys! Hundreds of Elves making countless toys! There was every kind of toy.

I was again dumbfounded. I stood with my mouth open until a finger flicked in and out of it again. I looked down into two beaming eyes, bright as stars. "Like it?" she said a flashed the biggest smile I have ever seen on any face.

"Like it? I love it. How...? Who...?" I felt like a child who had just seen my first toy. "Quickly my love, we have an audience with the council — this way, 'Saint' Nicholas."

"Oh phshaw," I replied, a little embarrassed. Then, realizing what she had said I asked, "What council?"

"So many questions!" She pulled me now, by the hand. "Answers later — Council now." We stepped into a large room with a completely circular table. In the center, above the table, was a holoscan. In the holoscan was a large assembly of several hundred beings, different life forms, all assembling together. Then, in a moment, the entire assembly grew quiet. A wise and gentle Elf rose to his feet and spoke.

"Nicholas and Crystal, the Galactic Council welcomes you to its midst. From now on you shall be full members of the council." The entire assembly rose and clapped their hands or made sounds that filled the holoscan. "As members you are recognized as Senders." Another loud applause as the assembly showed its appreciation. "You are herein bound by directives and principles as are all those who are Senders. Do you accept this appointment?"

I was wondering what the directives might be but Crystal stepped right up and said "Yes." She was holding my arm and, when I hesitated, she squeezed.

I responded, "Yes. Yes! I do." Again the assembly clapped and clapped. It was a standing ovation. As they finally quieted down, he continued.

"We are very concerned about the growing Grid of Agony on planet Earth and are pleased that you and the Elves have begun the Elfin project. This is a new experiment for us and we are watching it both with support and with hope. The black hole, as you know, is just beyond the shell of the cosmic egg of our space-time and has already succeeded in cracking the shell once." A great murmur arose from the assembly.

"Thanks to your efforts in putting the disc, infused with the love frequency of the Master Sender; and thanks also to the valiant efforts of your Elfin friends — Comcom, Misty, Doray, Mefa, Solah, and Tedo — and to the flying ability of the Griffin reindeer, you were able to seal the hole." A great applauding filled the assembly. After a time he was able to continue.

"We also understand that Delpha and her armada would have collapsed this entire galaxy into a new black hole, if you had not intervened once again." Once again, the assembly filled the holoscan with applause.

"In league with the Master Sender, you were able to reverse the threat of the black hole bomb and, as a result, a new star was born in our galaxy. For all this we, the council, congratulate you and your fellow workers." The assembly rose and began to chant words I could not understand. "Yes, yes. Just a moment," the Elf gestured.

The applause was so long I grew embarrassed. I felt like I was just along for the ride and I missed my family. As if reading my mind the holoscan showed, in one section of the assembly, my father in his fullest prime. Seated beside him was a woman who I assumed must be my mother. I began to move toward them but Crystal held my arm, "Later Nicholas. You will see them when this is done." I turned my attention back to the council.

"The council would like to congratulate the Sender Crystal." A great roar of approval filled the holoscan. After the assembly had calmed itself, he continued. "Not only was she able to serve as the channel for the tractor-beam that brought Nicholas, the Elves and the reindeer back from the edge of the black hole..." he was interrupted by another burst of applause. "But she has proven herself as an adept Sender when she delivered the love-infused toys to both the ancestors of Malevolent and Benton and," he hesitated because again the applause was so overwhelming, "she broke the Grid of Agony!"

Everyone in the assembly was on their feet cheering! Crystal just hung her head. It was me who was beaming! I was so proud of her. Never had I imagined I could love anyone so deeply as I did her at that moment. Here, standing beside me, was the love of my life, the person I knew was meant to walk beside me, my helpmate, my soul mate, my eternal love. I lifted our arms up in salute to the assembly. The cheering continued. At last they settled down. "And last, but not least, it was Crystal who helped design and now manages Elfin world at the North Pole!"

As the applause rose to another crescendo, I realized it was true. I was so honored to be with her. "We now, officials of the Galactic Council, now commission you both, Nicholas and Crystal, to work with the Elves in the Elfin project."

A great silence fell upon the assembly. They were listening. He continued. "We decided that, since the Delovians have broken the intergalactic directive and have intervened in Earth life by seeding the Grid of Agony and causing it to grow, it is only fair that Elves should respond to help humans take counter measures. We hereby grant you the right to *travel in time*, for as long as it takes, to seed the Grid of Agony with the Field of Love. This will neutralize the effect of the Delovians. It will depend upon the free will choice of all those involved, humans included. Do you accept this charge?"

"Will the Grid of Agony be completely destroyed by our efforts?" Crystal jerked my arm. "I want to know," I whispered in her ear.

"The ultimate state of planet Earth depends upon its inhabitants," he said. "If humans choose to live in agony, they may do so. Your commission is to neutralize the effects of the Delovian interference. If you do your job well, humans will always be able to choose love or agony."

"I accept," I said. "I too accept," she said. It took ten full minutes before the applause and the cheering died down.

"Go in peace, Nicholas, hereafter called 'Santa' and Crystal, the Senders." The holoscan closed to the roar of applause. The Elves were cheering and dancing for joy.

"Nicholas," she cooed. "Do you know what day it is?" I did not know even what month it was. "It's December, Nicholas. December 24, and we must plan our first major entry point into the grid."

I looked around me. Misty, Comcom, Doray, Mefa, Solah, Tedo and their team of Elves, all scattered throughout the amazing community, working to their hearts content, filled me with such a joy of life so full I laughed a deep belly laugh, "Ho, Ho, Ho!" This was my life! This was my work! To seed the Grid Agony with the Field of Love! To be a Sender and to make a difference on the planet.

The Elves were talking: "Every parent has the potential to release themselves from the habits of their inherited anguish by giving their children toys of love. It means we must find an entry point in the life of the parent, sometime before they were abused. Every abusive person was, at one time, a person before abuse took place."

"Notice how it worked in the life of Nicholas. He's even trying to be in love and we thought he would never be able to do it because part of his heart was still frozen by the abuse he suffered when his father was killed. We can find an entry point for the main characters in anyone's agony." I listened to their planning and smiled at Crystal.

"We did it with Malevolent and Benton." As they talked, I drew Crystal away. We walked through the forest together, alone at last.

"You know," she said, "we found the point of entry for Malevolent by reading the memory banks in his hair."

"In his hair." I reached up and twirled a lock of her hair in my fingers. "Hmmm." I looked at her hair.

"In his hair," she repeated. "It was the same with Benton. Evidently the microtubules of every cell in the body contain all the information of the body, including," she said as she turned and pointed at me, "the entire memory banks of the past. The Elves are able to read it through their holoscan." She turned again to walk with me. "It wouldn't have happened without the help of the children from the monastery." We walked a little way further, among the huge trees, smelling the flowers, just being together and being one.

"Those children were simply amazing. How did you get the hair from them?" I innocently asked.

"Well, I sneaked in one night, when the Priests least expected it…"

"YOU SNEAKED IN? What do you mean you SNEAKED in?" It was incredulous. "If they had found you…" my voice trailed off. I was thinking of the torture chamber but she giggled. I turned and I was serious. "I couldn't imagine what they would have done to you."

"Don't get chauvinistic on me," she giggled. "Women can do things, too, you know. I was small enough to get through the pond opening into the volcanic pit. Then I jumped a ride on one of the buckets." "You went up the bucket windlass?" I almost fainted.

"Yes, she said. "And the kids took the garments from both Malevolent and Benton and gathered samples of their hair. They put them in special pouches I gave to them and we got access to their memory banks. Pretty good, huh?"

I must have stood there with my mouth open again because her finger flicked in and out of it. "That could get to be a habit," she giggled.

"What about the guards?" I stormed.

"Oh, only one seemed to notice and I sort of helped him down the walkway with my levitator. He didn't wake up while I was there and no one said anything. I guess he was embarrassed to have tripped that way — especially when it happened the next night too." She grinned slyly at me.

I didn't know what to say and then, like a child, I cried rather meekly, "Don't you ever do that again!" Then, realizing what I had just said, I laughed. "I am going to have to watch you very carefully, I can tell." I took her in my arms.

"The Elves figured it right. Create a toy, infuse it with love and create a warp in the Grid. Allow the seed of love to be planted. It can change the past and dissolve the Grid of Agony." She just lay resting against my chest, our arms around each other.

"How did you figure out where to enter the past?" I was curious. "Well," she said, "it was a natural thing. I just looked at the time line and located the point at which the grid began to grow faster. We knew it had to be done before the acceleration point."

"But what about choosing the toy? How did you decide on the boat?" I was fascinated by the way her mind worked.

"Well, the Grid was dependent upon the agony caused by water. The whole thing started when Malevolent's father was thrown into the pond. So it was natural to find a way to help the child prepare for the challenge ahead of time. What better way to prepare to handle water that to give a boy a boat and let him learn about water by playing with a boat?" She looked up at me and gave me a quick peck on the cheek.

"How, then, did the boat get delivered? I thought only Senders can travel in time." Then, as if I was really stupid, I realized, "Oh, I get it."

She just kept on talking as if I were still normal. "The Elves knew that when you gave me the doll, the love frequencies infused my being and awoke the Sender in me."

I nodded my head, understanding and appreciating, more than I could say, the wonder of her.

"The Elves knew that everyone can be a Sender. It's inherent in our being."

We snuggled a little and then she whispered "It's a matter of choice. You can choose love…" and she bit the bottom of my ear just enough to rouse me from the warmth of our nest.

"So you and the Elves entered into Malevolent's past and seeded the Grid with a boat infused with love. That is amazing. When Malevolent's grandfather was still a child." "It was the best entry point. It had to start before he was abused and thrown into the pond." She continued. "It carries on from one generation to the next." We walked on a few steps. "OK, so we know that love is the most enduring thing on the planet." She raised her eyebrows. "I know our love is." I took her once again in my arms. I knew we had to plan our Christmas network of entry points but somehow this was all part of it.

"We got Malevolent by seeding his grandfather's life when he was playing beside the pond. Later, when his grandfather had already learned to swim, he loved being in the water. He won the pride of his father and became a very different man. Did you know he made toys as a hobby later in his life? His specialty was boats and, later, when his own son cried, he would put him in a tub of warm water and give him a boat to play with. It always worked."

It was incredulous to me and my face must have showed it. "Seriously, the Elves and I watched it on the holoscan. The Elves were really pleased." After a moment she added, "And Benton's parents — a book. It worked in both cases. The grid cannot defend itself against an infusion of genuine love."

"We can't get samples of hair from every child," I countered. "We can't holoscan everyone's life and then make an entry point someplace in the past." I began to realize how complex our work might become if we had to evaluate every child's life and enter into their past to correct the problem.

"Did you know that Benton's father never took a drink in his life?" I was still thinking about how to decide on an entry point. "After reading the book, the couple raised the child together and worked through their problems. Benton became a mason. He helps out at the Monastery. He and Malevolent are buddies. They have a special school at the Monastery for chil-

145

dren."

"That is amazing," I mused still focused on the entry point problem. "How can history just change?" I wondered aloud.

"Perhaps," she cooed, "it's all taking place in parallel worlds." I was stopped by the thought. "You mean..."

"Perhaps," she cooed again. And then, as if to completely leave the thought until another time, she said, "Something else I want to show you." By this time we were back at the starship.

As we entered, she jumped to the holoscan. The scene she pulled up was one with Priests at my father's workshop. One of the helpers was Benton. The scar on his face was gone. The scene scanned back to when the priests first approached the smithy shop. It looked like the inquisition was in full process and I was about to pull my head out of it, not wanting to experience it again. But Crystal took hold of my arm and said, "Wait. Don't go. I want you to see this." I waited.

I watched myself as I returned from my first visit with the Elves. I watched as I skipped across the field and my father gleefully shot the puffer into the air. Then the priests came from their hiding places and surrounded my father and I. Then I watched as Malevolent took charge.

"Why, these are toys!" he declared. "Toys!" declared Benton. "Why here's a boat!" They continued to examine the toys. "This is ingenious work! Look at this box."

He asked if it was all right to turn the key. My father nodded and watched with a smile on his face as Malevolent turned the key and listened to the music as the little dancers went round and round. "Think of what the children in the monastery would do with toys like these!"

As the priests took part in playing with the various toys, the paper floating planes, the parachute puffer, even the arrow and the puffer with my belt and buckle were appreciated for their potential good. I watched as everyone made plans to use the toys in teaching the children to love life, to explore reality and create a better future. "We can set up a whole new way to educate children," Malevolent exclaimed.

I turned as the Elves entered. They were filled with glee. "You made it!" said Comcom. "You are back. The Grid is fractured. The life crystal is growing. We are free!" All thoughts of parallel worlds were forgotten.

As everyone celebrated, I fished in my pocket for the ring. Suddenly, just as I was about to pull Crystal aside, Doray interrupted everyone's reverie with a grid alert. We all gathered around the holoscan. "One of the Elfin starships has been shot down by the U.S. Air Force." The silence was audible.

"When?" asked Comcom. "The earth year 1972," Mefa almost shouted. "Let's view it on the holoscan," he instructed as he moved to the screen. The holoscan immediately show the scene.

"The grid is overloaded with anguish. It is a time of war!" Doray observed. The holoscan shows as the explorer disc is sighted and taken for an enemy plane. It was shot down without any consideration. "One Elf lives. The other has passed on."

A great sense of loss settled over the Elfin Project. Then, from some deep place inside myself, I suggested, "Look for an entry point!" Like an electric shock, the Elves leaped into action.

"A total of 185 minds are involved in the shoot-down," reports Doray. "It will be the biggest project we have ever undertaken. It means we must find the gunner, the commanding officer, the government officials and the secret service agents who are involved in the public cover-up."

"We might as well get started," I said as I clutched the little cloth-covered packet in my pocket. "It means we must mobilize a multiple entry program timed in the early fifties. We might even be able to get amplified results."

Mefa reported: "It may take entry after entry to get the specific field to shift."

"It will require getting the U.S. Air Force Command ready for an interchange with the Elfin project. Somehow we must get the military to change from the basic premise that "war is inevitable" to the real premise that "unfolding life potential is inevitable," replied Comcom.

"Yes," said Misty. "We could seed the field so that the military changes from a 'war room' mentality to a 'peace room' mentality."

"But how can we know who to send toys to at any given moment?" Crystal exclaimed. "There is no way to know! So we have to think of a way to do the most good with what time we have available." It was her words that triggered my next thought.

"Time is not the problem. We can travel in time." We were both silent for a moment and then I got it. "Well then," I said, "we must deliver toys to every child." Everyone agreed. It was an immense project. I participated for some time and then, noticing Crystal was no longer with us, I stepped away from the Starship and all its intensity.

It was Christmas Eve. While the Elves and their committees brainstormed the details of the next time travel, I passed through the forest and came to the cottage that the Elves had made for Crystal. It was tucked in among the ferns and trees of the forest, away from the hustle and bustle of the toy-making factory. The light in her bedroom glowed gently in the shadows of the evening. She had collapsed upon her bed and had fallen asleep.

This was my night of nights. I slipped quietly into her bedroom and sat down quietly beside her. I brushed a curl of her hair from her forehead with my hand. She stirred as I looked upon her in her sleep. She seemed that most beautiful and desirable being in the universe as far as I could tell.

I pulled the cloth from my pocket and unfolded it. The ring was there, glowing in the faint light. I lifted the ring and gently took hold of her hand. She woke then, almost as if in a dream, she took me in her arms and kissed me so lovingly, so longingly and so completely that I forgot about the ring. "I love you, Nicholas Claus." And then she swooned, "alias Kris Kringle and Santa the Sender."

"I love you Crystal... Hey, what is your last name?" I had never thought of taking the time to ask. We both laughed and, searching around for the ring, she jumped and giggled. Finally finding the ring, I said, "Would you agree to it being 'Claus'?"

She looked at the ring and took it lovingly in her hands. "Why Nicholas!" she exclaimed, "it is a work of art!" She looked up at me with such loving eyes. "You have been busy in your spare time!" She looked carefully at the ring. "This is absolutely beautiful — the sleigh and the reindeer!" Then she noticed something written inside the ring. "What's this?" She began to laugh. "You are the most amazing being I have ever met," she laughed. "Three magic words!" I just blushed a little and mumbled, "It says 'HO! HO! HO!'" She giggled, "Perrrrrfect!" as I took the ring and fit it on her finger. "Will you marry me?" she asked.

I laughed. "Those are supposed to be my words!" She pulled me down upon the bed. "I'd like to stay," I said, "but I have a little trip to make." As I rose from the bed, she laughed and threw back the covers. She was fully dressed in a red cashmere outfit, white trim and black belt. She slipped on her boots as she said, "I am coming with you." When she saw me hesitate, she explained, "I have everything organized. The factory is completed, the toys are in order and the Elves know exactly what needs to be done. In fact, we have more toys than we can deliver this year. I am coming with you. Besides, I am already experienced at delivering toys on the sleigh." We both laughed.

As we entered the factory, the Elves were all excited. "The light crystal is finished," Comcom explained. It is time for us to continue our journey. Before we leave, allow us to gift you with our gift of love."

The Elves took us then and placed us upon the central control disc above their life crystal. They gathered around us and Misty stepped forward. "As a gift to you, we are programming you to age only to the prime of your lives..." "When you are most Elf-like!" chimed in Mefa.

"So you can maintain for all time, the shape of loving Senders. Your cells will respond so the harmonic remains stable. You two will never die."

In the silence of the moment, Crystal leaned over and whispered, "It means we get to have an ongoing purposeful relationship." We all laughed in the joy of knowing each other and the work we would be doing for as long as time exists.

There before us stood our remarkable friends, the Elves: Misty, Comcom, Doray, Mefa, Solah and Tedo. They circled us and joined hands as Comcom stepped forward. I took Crystal's hand and Comcom placed his three-fingered hands upon each of our shoulders. Looking directly into my eyes he said:

"Open the portals of time. Seed the Grid of Agony with love. Shift the field from fear to love. Transform the past and create the future now. Be the Sender. The Grid of Agony grows. You will need more Senders. Call them. They will come. Let them gather together and transform the Grid of Agony into a Field of Love. Preserve life on this planet. All that is required, you have."

He gently, so gently, removed his aged three fingered hands from my shoulders. Too much living in time had aged him. His great almond eyes held mine for a moment and in that moment I could see a thousand lives so clearly it was as though I had lived them as my own. Life after life after life and lesson upon lesson upon lesson swept before me as my mind leapt to the realization of love so profound, of peace so universal that it had woven the very fabric of time and space and birthed the source from which life sprang.

A river of light burst from my heart, washing through every cell of my body, lifting, cleansing, transforming the ashes of my agony, freeing and centering me. Suddenly I was back again to the days of my youth working with my father in his toyshop, yet filled with a joy unspeakable.

As he turned to leave, his parting words echoed over and over in my heart. "You are the Sender. Send for the others." Then he was gone, his starship dissolving into the vastness of inner space.

I am the Sender Nicholas, known as Santa Claus. This is the story of my adventures with the Elves and of how they taught me to transform the Grid of Agony by seeding it with Field of Love and saved life on planet earth.

This is the story of how Crystal, my beloved companion, and the Elves, created the Elfin Project near the North Pole and how we created a great factory for the manufacturing of toys infused with love. So, every Christmas Eve, at precisely midnight, now or in a thousand years, past or future, we travel in time in our red sleigh pulled by eight tiny reindeer and deliver toys fused with love from the Master Sender. In this way we seed the Grid of Agony with the Field of Love.

From the Elves and from the Galactic Council, from the Master Sender and from all Senders everywhere, we, Nicholas and Crystal Claus, send this message:

Live love now! Allow love! Embrace love! Become love! Love one another! Share gifts of love with each other! Be Senders! Send love! Transform the Grid of Agony into the Field of Love! Call for the Senders! Hold the Field of Love in the present! Send love into the past and project love into the future! Love all people! Love all life! Align with your fullest potential S-Elves! Be the love you are and manifest the love we are in all dimensions! Love works. Live love now…

AND BE SURE TO HAVE A VERY

MERRY CHRISTMAS!

For thousands of years legends of Elves have been passed on in various cultures. Who, for example, were the Elves that assisted St. Nicholas and, as legend tells us, helped create toys for children and assisted in the celebration of Christmas? Where did they come from? How did they become involved with this planet? Why did they end up working with humans? Why did they start to build toys? In this, his first science novel, Dr. Woolf outlines an amazing adventure of a young boy who is drawn into a galactic war between two dimensions of reality: dark matter and the visible universe.

The boy is thrust into the depths of the power of darkness that controlled the inquisitions of the 15 century and, quite by accident, comes into possession of the powerful dark crystal that opens the portal to other dimensions invisible to others. The plan of the Delovians, who rule in the dimensions of dark matter, is to create a global grid of agony among humans. The purpose of the grid is to draw physical matter into a black hole and convert it into dark matter for Delovian use. Their plan is discovered and only through the direct intervention of the Elves does life have any chance of continuing on earth.

Intervention requires the creation of a *Field of Love,* which can only be accomplished by direct human action. The adventure that Nicholas has with the Elves leads the reader through half a dozen enfolded dimensions of reality and unveils the secrets to transforming agony into love. This is a message that applies to everyone's daily life. It's for children and adults and provides not only the tools for the transformation of the powers of darkness, but also opens the doors to an entirely new perspective about Christmas.

Victor Vernon Woolf's phenomenal book Holodynamics: How to Develop and Manage your Personal Power and his worldwide training programs on Unfolding Potential introduced millions of people to the hidden dimensions of consciousness and showed people how to use this information to solve some of the most complex problems on the planet.

Now, in a major publishing event, Dr. Woolf returns with a detailed sequel that unravels the mysteries of how people were able to solve not only their own personal problems but also how to transform the drug abuse culture in six cities, hard-core criminals in prison, overcome dysfunctional corporate and government dynamics, and even end war. After a 15-year absence, in which he had a major impact in the ending of the Cold War and helping to restructure Russia and the Republics, he now returns to show how this information has been able to transform even terrorism in the Middle East.

One of the most profound thinkers and teachers of our time, Dr. Woolf has become an icon in the world of consciousness, not only for his adventures in solving complex problems around the world, but also for his humor and unique approach in the integration of what is known from science -- especially the new sciences -- and how this new information applies to human consciousness. In this new book, The Dance of Life, Dr. Woolf takes us into the cutting edge of physics, biology, neurology, holographics and information theory. With pictures, cartoons and stories, we explore the secrets of how we can effectively transform both individual and collective consciousness.

Few people in history have demonstrated the effectiveness of their approach in such practical ways. When he talks about transforming your world NOW, resolving conflicts, and harmonizing your "Being" with nature, it is not just talk. He has already accomplished these objectives. This text has five Manuals that provide more details and exercises in the practical application of this information.

In this book, Dr. Woolf invites the reader to participate in an extraordinary voyage into the deepest enfolded dimensions of reality and into the source and network of consciousness itself. In great detail, we journey through the dimensions of the consciousness of nature and of humans. Different dimensions of consciousness show why people experience reality in different ways and why conflicts occur and how they can be resolved. This book is a practical journey into more conscious living in a conscious universe. It holds the keys to a more sustainable future. The veils of consciousness are lifted to reveal a multidimensional reality more intricate and amazing than any of us ever imagined.

Dr. Woolf is a recognized world trainer, speaker and consultant. He is a member of the Russian Academy of Natural Sciences and Director of the International Academy of Holodynamics and has received many awards including the Academy of natural Science's top award for "outstanding contributions to science and society" in 1996.

His background in physics, education, religion and psychology established an integrated approach to consciousness that was the basis for his remarkable record of successes.